HIDDEN
HEART

Book Two of The Hidden Trilogy

Amy Patrick

Visit http://www.amypatrickbooks.com/ to sign up for Amy's newsletter if you would like to receive news and insider information on The Hidden Trilogy books and release dates.

CONTENTS

PROLOGUE

It was her, or at least it might have been her, if she'd cut her hair and gotten major highlights, which she probably had. The girl turned and I saw her face. Another false alarm.

It was my first big Hollywood party, and I was the lame zebra trying to keep up with the stampeding herd, moving through a sea of designer dresses, and beautiful faces, and crystal champagne flutes. Emmy was here somewhere. She had to be, because if she wasn't, I'd have no idea where else to look.

Having already searched the first three floors of the massive, glass-walled modern art museum of a house, I walked out onto the roof deck where the sounds of a slick alternative band filled the moist salty air, pumping up the party guests to an even higher pitch.

Scanning the scene, I finally spotted what I was looking for—not Emmy, but the next best thing. The one person who knew for sure where she was, where she'd been the past few weeks. He was leaning against the balcony railing, his perfect form framed by a backdrop of stars over the Malibu beach, and naturally, surrounded by a crowd of adoring teenage girls and twenty-something women.

Adrenaline surged through my veins like the surf pounding in the background. Finally, after everything I'd gone through to get here, I was so close to finding her.

Preparing to charge Vallon Foster—huge Elven bodyguards be damned—I planned to demand Emmy's whereabouts and immediate release. A strong hand gripped my shoulder and slid down to my waist. I was pulled back against the solid warmth of a large male body.

"Calm down, Ryann," a smooth familiar voice murmured at my ear. "And let me handle this."

With considerable effort, I reeled in my emotions and pasted on a smile. We approached the movie star together, hand in hand.

"Sweetheart, I'd like you to meet my good friend, Vallon Foster." The voice of the beautiful guy beside me was comforting, full of loving assurance.

I forced myself to appear something less-than-hostile as Nox introduced me.

"Vallon, this is Ryann… the newest member of my fan pod."

CHAPTER ONE
GUARDIAN

One month earlier

Nox walked beside me, keeping up, seemingly oblivious to the fact I was ignoring him. I was embarrassingly winded from my attempt to leave him behind, but naturally, he was unaffected by the brisk pace. I slid a narrowed glance to the side.

"You really can't take a hint, can you?"

Glancing over at me with a half-smile, he said, "No, I understand very well you'd rather be with anyone else on the planet right now. But I'm still not letting you walk home alone."

I gestured toward the peaceful woods surrounding us, the sun-dappled leaves, the quiet underbrush, the dusty narrow path leading to Grandma Neena's log house. "This is ridiculous. I've walked alone on my grandma's land a million times. I think I can manage to make it back to the house in the middle of the day without a chaperone."

Nox shook his head. "You don't know what's going on back there in Altum. Things are crazy. Besides, I'm only following orders from your *beloved* Lad—my new king."

I shot him a dirty look and attempted to walk even faster as if that would make it more difficult for him to keep up. "Just... don't talk, okay? I don't want to hear anything you have to say."

"Fine." Nox dropped back a step but stayed at my heels for the remainder of the brittle, silent march.

Reaching the steps of Grandma Neena's back porch, I attempted to go inside without another word to Nox. He was in front of me and blocking the door before I could get a foot past the threshold.

"I'm coming in." His tone said *deal with it.*

I laughed in his face. "You most certainly are not. You carried out your orders—now get lost."

"Lad said to take care of you."

"He *said* to take me home, and now I'm home. Goodbye."

His eyes narrowed and a grin sneaked across his face. "Well, if you want to be perfectly technical about it, Ryann, he said 'take her.' There could be many interpretations of that particular phrase... if you'd care to start exploring them."

My face burned at his raised eyebrow, insinuating tone, and annoying persistence—so familiar—so infuriating. I pushed at his chest, and he stepped back, allowing me into the kitchen.

"Go away, Nox. I don't need a babysitter, and I really don't want to spend any more time talking to someone whose native language is lies."

Shutting the door, he turned to face me, his dark hair messy and curling where it touched the tops of his ears, his intense hazel eyes imploring me for understanding. I glared back at him. Perhaps deciding not to waste his time arguing with me, he shrugged and simply walked past me into the living room, his large body brushing the front of mine as he passed.

He collapsed onto the brown leather couch, his long legs and arms flung out comfortably as if he was used to hanging out here after school every day. The scene was so unlike the first time Lad had come inside my house, the first and only time Lad had ever entered a human's house.

Was Nox this comfortable everywhere in the human world? His band, The Hidden, played a steady circuit of nightclubs and small concert halls. He ate all of his meals in restaurants or bars. He must have stayed in hotel rooms when they were on the road. We'd gone to school together this past year, but with all of that, did he have any human friends? Or was there only me?

As long as I'd known him, I'd naturally assumed him to *be* human. I didn't know anything about his Elven life, whether he still even lived in Altum. He'd been there earlier today, but that might have only been because the

Assemblage was going on—the gathering drew Elven tribes from across the continent every ten years.

I certainly wasn't going to engage him in further conversation about it. The only thing I wanted to talk about was his immediate departure.

"Are you moving in? Should I make up a bed for you?"

There was nothing playful in my sarcasm or rude tone, but he grinned at me anyway. "Yes, that would be lovely. And I think I'll have a snack, too. I'm starved." He rubbed his flat belly.

I gave him a saccharine smile. "How does a nice big plate of 'Get out' sound to you?"

Nox sat forward, resting his elbows on his knees. His deep hazel eyes looked up at me from under black brows. The smile dropped from his face, which suddenly looked tired.

"I told you Ryann—I'm supposed to take care of you. Things at Altum are... not good at the moment. It's chaos. Everyone's running around making accusations." A long pause. "Your name came up more than once."

Shock pushed all the breath out of my lungs. I dropped back into the chair behind me. "My name?" The words were a whisper. "So then, they're going to come after me?"

A fierce light came into his eyes, and his hands clasped together in front of him. "They might try. Don't worry. I'm not going to let anyone get near you. That's why I went to find you and Lad in your little love nest. I didn't want the two of you to come strolling back hand-in-hand. Who knows what would have happened to you?"

My palms came to the sides of my face, the gravity of the situation sinking in. "Poor Lad. Poor Mya. What could have happened?" I shivered in spite of the warmth of the room.

Nox shook his head, his shoulders sagging heavily. "I don't know. I'd just come back to Altum, I saw Lad running—I knew he was going after you—I told him where to find you, and he left. About ten minutes later, all Hell broke loose. Apparently, Ivar's servant found him in his room. His body was still warm. I didn't hear what else was said about that part—there was this sudden hurricane of thoughts flying around. Lad told you how we—yeah? Okay, well, all these questions and accusations were coming from every direction. 'Was it Audun? Lad himself? The human girl? The outcast Neena?'"

I lurched to my feet. "Grandma? Oh my God, Nox. I have to go to her—what if they—"

At the squeak of the back screen door opening, Nox sprang from the couch. Stepping in front of me, he stretched to his full six feet, four inches. He relaxed as Grandma entered the room from the kitchen.

Relief flooded her face as well. "Ryann. Thank God you're here."

I ran to my grandma, throwing my arms around her skinny shoulders. "Lad's father," I began, but she pulled back, and her face showed she knew already.

"It's terrible. I can't even believe it. After all this time... to see him again. And now he's *gone*."

"What happened? Were you there? Did someone really kill him? Maybe he had a heart attack or something?"

She shook her head. "No. Elves don't suffer from human diseases. Something violent must happen to end our lives and our immortality. Someone definitely did it. But they don't know who yet. I was in my family's quarters when it happened, but the news travelled quickly."

"Did you see Lad? Can you take me to him?"

She grabbed my upper arms and looked right into my eyes. "No, sweetheart. You must not go to Altum. *Ever* again. Not unless Lad himself takes you there when this is all over. It's not safe now."

"But—"

"I saw him—he told me to tell you to stay away. He'll come to you as soon as he's able."

"When?" My voice sounded panicky.

"He didn't say. He's got a lot to deal with, Ryann. Try to understand."

"I do understand. But it's so horrible, and he's hurting. I want to help him."

"You can—by staying away so he can do what has to be done without worrying about your safety." She glanced across the room, lifting her chin in Nox's direction. "What's he doing here?"

"Annoying me."

"Protecting her." Nox and I spoke at the same time, our words overlapping.

Grandma Neena wrapped her thin arm around my shoulder and nodded to Nox. "Thank you, son, but you can go now." As he began to protest, she continued. "We'll be fine. I don't think anyone will come, but I'll be aware of it if they do. You go on home."

I echoed her instructions but with considerably more enthusiasm. "Go, Nox. I don't need you."

He grimaced and didn't move, only stood completely still for a few moments with his hands clenching and unclenching, his lips pressed together, staring at me. Finally he went to the door and opened it, but he didn't step outside. He turned back, and our eyes met.

Later.

I heard the word in my mind as clearly as if he'd said it aloud. Then he walked out the door, slamming it behind him.

Grandma and I looked at each other. "That was your friend Nox? The boy you've been spending time with? When you spoke of him, I had no idea he was Elven."

"You and me both," I grumbled.

"What happened between you two?" she asked.

"Nothing. Nox walked me home, and I tried to get him to leave, but he was being stubborn about it. He says I'm under suspicion in Altum for Ivar's murder. And you might be, too. Is it true?"

She nodded with a grim expression before turning to go into the kitchen. Opening the refrigerator and pulling out the tea pitcher, she gestured for me to sit at the old farm table. "I'm afraid it is. Not about me—I was in my family's quarters with them, so I have an alibi. But about you—yes. That's why you mustn't try to go back there. Promise me you won't. Even if… even if he never comes to you. Even if you never see him again. I'm not even sure if it's safe for us to stay here."

"No." I practically shouted the word. More quietly, I said, "I'm not going anywhere. And he *will* come. We're together now. We *have* to be together."

Grandma dropped the plastic tumbler she'd taken from a cabinet and whirled around. Her face was white. "You didn't bond with him, did you?"

Heat flooded my cheeks and ears as my gaze dropped to the scarred wooden tabletop. "No. We didn't. But we're in love. We're together now. And Ivar said—"

Standing right in front of me now, Grandma Neena said, "Ivar is dead, sweetheart. Everything is different now—for my people—certainly for Lad, and most likely for you, too. I'm sorry to say it, but I don't want you to be surprised."

"Surprised?"

"If Lad… ends things between you."

I jumped up from my chair, heart hammering at the suggestion. "No. That will never happen." Her answering look of sympathy drove me from the room.

In my own room behind closed doors, I paced and worried until I thought I might go crazy. I left the curtains wide open and obsessively checked the darkening window every few minutes for fireflies or any other sign of Lad's arrival. Climbing into bed, I opened a favorite book to occupy my mind until he came to me, as I knew he would. *He will. He has to.*

After reading the same paragraph four times in a row, I finally gave up on the book and turned on the television. A re-run of a popular crime drama was on, and though I'd never been a huge fan, I recognized the actors. For the first time, I studied them—their idealized faces, their long muscular limbs in perfect proportion to their remarkable height. It was so obvious to me now the majority of the people on the screen were not human, but Elven.

Ignorant that Elves even existed, I'd never realized before how many actors, and musicians, and athletes, and even political leaders displayed the unnaturally perfect physical attributes of Elves.

And the glamour they all possessed—the glamour Dark Elves freely used on humans—well, it was no wonder celebrity worship was overtaking society, dominating social media and newscasts, and even the conversations of my closest friends.

Which brought me to Emmy. Unless I found a way to stop her, in a few weeks she'd be leaving to join Vallon Foster's fan pod in Los Angeles. One more reason I needed to see Lad again as soon as possible.

Though he was a Light Elf, he certainly knew more about Dark Elves than I did. Together we'd find a way to protect Emmy. Together we'd deal with his family's tragedy.

Together. We have to be together.

When midnight came and Lad still hadn't come, I finally turned off my lamp and went to pull the curtains. I startled as my eye caught a flash of movement high in a tree at the edge of the yard. My heart leapt. Lad. He's here.

Then I heard his voice. Not Lad's. Nox's.

Sleep. You're safe.

Nox was concealed just inside the tree line, watching over the house.

That didn't make me feel safe. It made me uncomfortable. I didn't need him, and I didn't want him.

I wasn't sure if my own fledgling Elven communication skills were up to the task, but I sent him a return message.

Not with you.

CHAPTER TWO
FINISHED

The summer before my senior year should have been my happiest yet, but instead I felt like I was sleepwalking through it. Day after day passed with no word from Lad, and I went through the motions while my mind stayed fixed on him. I could barely stand it, waiting, worrying, not knowing what he was doing, how he was doing.

Days, I worked at The Skillet. Nights, I went to the ballpark with Emmy and Shay—I was trying to spend as much time as possible with Emmy before she left for Los Angeles to join the fan pod.

Actually I needed to find a way to *keep* her from going. All my efforts to persuade her against it so far had failed epically. My celeb-obsessed lifelong friend was more determined than ever, and she'd said if we were going to *remain* friends, I'd better not make any more negative remarks about her dream-come-true plans.

If only I could tell her the truth about *why* I was afraid for her—that she'd be unknowingly enslaving herself to a Dark Elf. They were different from Light Elves—they considered themselves superior to humans and longed for the days when humans would once again serve and worship them. And based on the way they surrounded themselves with young, attractive fan pod members, they didn't bond the same way—limiting themselves to one partner for life.

"Admit it—he broke your heart," Emmy said when she spotted Nox's car pulling into the ballpark one night in late June. Shay nodded in agreement as if this was a subject the two of them had discussed.

"That is *so* not true," I protested. Nox *hadn't* broken my heart. He had broken something just as difficult to repair—my trust. "We were only friends."

Being my best friend since preschool, Emmy had naturally picked up on my near-constant funk. But I couldn't explain to her—or anyone—what had happened with Lad, so I couldn't blame her for trying to fill in the blanks. She and Shay assumed I was depressed about the obvious rift in my relationship with Nox.

"Sure, okay," she said, clearly unconvinced.

I couldn't explain the truth about Nox either. I couldn't say anything that might expose his secret—Lad's secret. Protecting it was the number one rule of the Elven race. Revealing it could put Lad and all his people—possibly Emmy, too—in danger. Even if I *could* have told her, she would've thought it was just another attempt to keep her from pursuing her dream. Who would actually believe such a crazy thing?

"Well, he broke *Savannah's* heart. They only dated for a week, and I swear the girl hasn't been the same since. He must be some kind of addictive substance," Shay commented, craning her neck to see Nox getting out of his car and sounding like she wouldn't mind a hit herself.

"So, are you all packed for cheer camp tomorrow?" I asked her, trying to change the subject.

"You know it. And I go right to Girls' State after that, so I'm going to be gone for three weeks. What about you?" She gave Emmy a shoulder bump. "You must be counting down the minutes by this point."

Emmy nodded vigorously, hopping as she spoke. "Three more days! In *three* days I'll be basking in the California sun, mingling with celebrities, and meeting *Vallon Foster*. Can you believe it?"

"No," I said, shaking my head.

Shay gave me an elbow nudge to the ribs, and smiling widely, overcompensated for my lack of approval. She wasn't quite as into the whole fan pod hype as Emmy was, but she didn't share my objections and thought I was being a little harsh about the whole thing. She was supportive of Emmy's plans and full of contagious excitement.

"It's amazing! You have to text us all the time and post pics every day. I wish I was going with you—"

"No you don't," I interrupted before I could stop myself.

15

Both of them looked at me like I was unbalanced. Emmy's crestfallen expression made my heart twist in my chest. She thought I was being a bad friend.

"You promised... I support you about your tea company thing. You support Shay about her cheering and student government stuff."

"Sorry," I said, but I didn't mean it, and of course she could tell. There was no way she could understand what was behind my negative attitude about the fan pods. Cheerleading camp and leadership camp were temporary. Shay would be home safe in a few weeks. Emmy might *never* come home again. Not as the same girl anyway. Maybe not even alive.

Shay let out an uncomfortable laugh. "Okay, we know Ryann's not a super-fan. But we're all happy for each other, right?" Grabbing each of our hands, she pulled us into a little impromptu friend-circle right there near the snack bar. "Let's just enjoy these last few days we have together, okay y'all?"

We all smiled and agreed, and I resolved once again to keep my worry to myself while finding a way to save Emmy somehow. As she'd noted, I had three days left. Maybe I could call in a bomb scare and ground her flight to L.A.?

My fear for her—for Lad—for *us*—was making me a wreck. When I could finally manage to fall asleep each night, it was fitful and full of nightmares. Often my dreams featured eyes staring from the woods—not beautiful leaf-green eyes like Lad's, but harsh accusing Elven eyes, and worse—mysterious hazel ones.

Each day I grew more exhausted. I begged Grandma to go back to Altum and check on Lad for me, but she refused, saying it was better for all of us to follow his no-contact order, that he would come to me when it was safe or would let us know if it became too unsafe for us to remain in our home.

"Guess who's coming this wa-ay," Shay crooned, teasing me.

I glanced in the direction of her gaze and frowned at the sight of Nox's long, lazy stride bringing him closer. Since the day he'd escorted me home, our only interaction had been when he brought deliveries of saol water from Altum, where it was produced, so I could continue using it to flavor and sweeten my special recipe tea. Whether he'd been selected—or volunteered himself as delivery boy—I wasn't sure.

I had only a few months to get the Magnolia Sugar Tea Company up and running and producing enough gourmet sweet tea to stock a hundred and ten Food Star grocery stores across the southeast. Working to get the business operational had been a godsend as far as keeping my mind occupied.

When my facility eventually came on-line and my production increased, I'd need large amounts of saol water, but I knew I'd always have a steady supply—the fate of the Light Elves' home rested on it—thus the regular deliveries.

Nox approached the three of us, wearing his trademark cocky grin. No doubt he anticipated a captive audience—not from me—he *knew* how I felt about him. When he came into the Skillet for meals these days, I made sure another waitress took his table. Late at night I sometimes spotted him keeping watch over the house in a tree on the border of Grandma's yard, but I couldn't do anything about that. The forest had belonged to the Elves long before my human ancestors moved here.

Nox came to a stop before us, nodding to Emmy, then Shay, then locking his eyes on mine, lifting a brow and offering his I'm-too-cute-to-hate smile. "A triangle. Can I join?"

The smooth, sexy purr caused an involuntary shiver and raised goosebumps on my skin. Shay and Emmy gave each other annoyingly knowing looks and stepped away, giggling, leaving us alone to talk. I scowled after them. They had no *idea* how much they *didn't* know about me and Nox.

Turning my attention to him, I sighed. "Keep dreaming, cowboy. What do you want?"

"Oh, wait a minute, I have a list." He pretended to dig through the pockets of his faded, perfectly-fitted jeans. "No, actually, I was hoping that since we're in public and outdoors and you can't slam the door in my face, you might give me a few minutes to talk to you—to explain. You *might* find yourself interested in what I have to say, as amazing as it might seem."

I would have loved to skewer him with a *drop-dead* stare, but the fact he was about six inches taller than me, not counting his black western boots, made that difficult. And I wasn't short in anybody's book. I gave it my best try anyway.

His grin only widened.

"Assuming I did decide to waste entire minutes of my life listening to your *explanation*, why should I believe anything you say ever again?"

He instantly dropped the grin and looked soberly right into my eyes, his expression turning intense. "Because I'll never lie to you again."

"You just did." I spun on my heel and looked back over my shoulder as I walked away to join my friends. "And don't bother with the pushy look. I'm surprised you haven't figured it out yet—the Sway doesn't work on me."

His stunned expression was the first thing to make me smile all day.

The next morning as I was getting ready for work there was a knock at the back door. Mom and Grandma had left already, so I went to answer it. Expecting to see Emmy or perhaps Nox making an unscheduled drop off, I yanked the door open.

And there was Lad, standing on the front porch.

Heart melting with relief, I shocked myself by bursting into tears. I ran to him and embraced him, expecting the vigorous wrapped-in-his-arms reception he usually offered.

Lad didn't move. Instead, he stood like an oak tree with his arms at his sides, allowing my embrace but not returning it. Confused, I stepped back and looked up at him.

His face was stoic and controlled, making him resemble a marble statue some master had carved and dropped off on our porch. Making him look like his father.

His gaze flickered over me, settling on my face. The unearthly green eyes were more beautiful than ever, but there was a coldness in them. I detected none of the emotion that had been there only two weeks ago when he'd said he was willing to leave his home and family behind for me.

As it turned out, that hadn't been necessary. His father had released Lad from a forced political marriage to the daughter of the Dark Elves' leader. Ivar had freed his son to come and find me and tell me the words I'd been longing to hear. *I love you.*

I inhaled his fresh, woodsy fragrance. God, he still smelled better than any human being I'd ever met. But something about him had definitely changed.

"Lad?" Was he not going to say anything at all? An anxious pulse thrummed in my neck as I waited.

He swallowed and finally spoke, his tone careful and polite. "Ryann. How have you been?"

I wanted to laugh. I wanted to scream. "How've I been? I've been desperately worried about you. I've been *miserable,* missing you and wondering if you're okay. Lad... how are *you?*" I stepped forward again and took his hands in mine.

He looked down at our fingers, mine small and pinkish-pale against his tanned complexion. When his eyes came up to meet mine, they were bright the way they used to be. Something intimate and alive flourished between us, a sense of connection returning. And then the clouds came back, blotting out the brightness and leaving me chilled by his once-again-distant expression.

He slipped his fingers out of mine. "I am well, thank you."

So formal. So un-Lad-like.

"I'm sorry it's taken so long for me to contact you, but I've had... responsibilities. Things are somewhat calmer now. A sense of order has been restored. My mother is still inconsolable, but... life goes on."

I stepped forward, desperate to be near him. "I'm so sorry. I don't know how to tell you how bad I feel for you and how much I've been wanting to be there for you. I've missed you so much."

It would have been natural at this point for Lad to tell me he'd missed me, too, for us to embrace and comfort each other. None of that happened. He just looked at me, his expression unreadable.

Taking a step back, he clasped his hands behind his back and lifted his chin. "I appreciate that. Well... I'm sure you're busy. You look like you're getting ready to go out."

"Don't be silly. I'll skip work."

"No. No, Ryann. That's not necessary. I only needed to see that you're okay—to tell you I believe it's safe for you and your family to remain here. You can go to work. I'm finished here."

Finished. What the heck did that mean? And his tone was so flat, so final. My heartbeats began multiplying, tripping over each other in a race toward a very bad conclusion.

"What do you mean, you're 'finished here?' I haven't seen you for two weeks, there's been a horrible tragedy in your family, we've talked for all of two minutes and now you're 'finished?' Like this was a chore you had to check off of your list today? Lad, so much has happened. Come in and sit down. We need to talk. We need to figure out what we're going to do now."

"Nothing."

"Nothing?"

"*We* are going to do nothing. My life—the life I dreamed of with you—is over now, Ryann. I am leader of Altum. It is my destiny, my responsibility. My feelings for you…" He faltered, closing his eyes and breathing in and out slowly before continuing, "My feelings no longer matter. My people need me. And though they don't realize it, your people also need me to be there, doing my duty. These are dangerous, dark times for us all."

I shivered with a chill in the warm summer air. "Dangerous. Who's in danger? You?"

"Perhaps. The humans are, certainly. And you. If you don't stay away from me—you are endangered most of all. You must never try to see me or speak to me again. You must forget about me, Ryann."

The breath left my lungs suddenly as if I'd been punched in the gut. "What? No. No, I can't do that. Why are you doing this?"

He shook his head sadly. "I wish you were susceptible to my glamour— then I could *force* you to forget you ever met me. The way it should have been from the beginning."

Pain radiated from my center out through my entire body. *How can he say that?* He didn't truly wish he'd never met me. He didn't really want me to forget about him, about us. Did he?

"Lad—this is a terrible, terrible time. But it's going to pass. You'll find out who killed your father. Justice will be done. Your mom will start to get better gradually—I've seen my mom overcome heartbreak—it's not easy, but your mother can do it, too. I know you need time to deal with everything that's happened. When things calm down, I'll still be here. I wish you'd let me be there for you, help you right now. But if not, I understand. It's okay. I'm not going anywhere. I love you—I'll wait for you as long as it takes."

Finally, some emotion warmed the frosty green eyes, some clue he cared one way or another about what I was saying. I saw a spark of hope and maybe… longing? But he refused to give anything away with his words.

"Don't wait, Ryann. There is no point in it. Live your life and be happy. That is my wish for you—though I cannot be a part of it." He gave me a sad smile, and in it I saw a shadow of the weariness and strain he must have been feeling nonstop for the past two weeks.

My heart ached for him. He was overwhelmed. He couldn't see past his current terrible circumstances, but he would in time. I was sure of it.

"Things worked out before—they will again, Lad. You'll see." I had to believe that.

He stood looking at me a moment longer, his eyes deep green and filled with finality. Then he kissed me on the forehead, turned, and descended the front steps, walking into the woods without another word.

Chapter Three
Vanishing Act

I needed to talk to Emmy. Mom had already left for work at the funeral home, and Grandma Neena was at her art class. If I didn't talk to someone soon, my brain was going to burst. And if anyone could give me advice or at least commiserate over a broken heart, it was Emmy. I knew she wouldn't be at work today—she wasn't on the schedule because she was leaving for L.A. in a couple of days. So I called her.

No answer. Probably running around making last minute preparations for her trip—a trip straight to a Hell disguised as fangirl heaven. I still hadn't come up with a way to keep her from going, and I was getting desperate. She was my best friend, and she was about to ruin her life. Elven rules or not, I might have to tell her the truth about the fan pods and the Dark Elves.

If *that* didn't stop her, I guessed I'd have to risk juvy and slash her parents' car tires to keep her from getting to the airport in Memphis. I didn't know how else to accomplish it at this point.

When my next attempt went right to Emmy's voicemail, I called in sick to work, telling Dory my stomach was queasy—which was absolutely true. I was starting to get a very bad feeling about all this.

As soon as Grandma pulled into the long gravel drive, I was out the door. I met the car as it rolled to a stop under the carport.

"Hi. Can I borrow your keys to go into town?" My question was breathless.

Her brow furrowed as she studied me. "Well, sure. Everything okay?"

"No. Not really. I don't know," I reached for the set of keys she offered. "That's what I need to find out. Lad broke up with me."

"Oh honey—I'm sorry."

"And I… I can't even think about it right now because Emmy's not answering her phone or my texts, and she's supposed to leave in two days. I'm afraid something's wrong."

"Oh dear. Well, tell me as soon as you find out what's happening. And we'll talk about Lad later." She gave me a look of complete understanding and watched as I climbed behind the wheel and backed out of the carport.

Emmy's mom came to the door when I knocked. She was all smiles. "Hey there, Ryann. What brings you by today?"

"Well, you know, I want to make sure I see Emmy before she leaves, and she's not answering her phone. She's not sick, is she?" I hoped my voice didn't sound too hopeful. A nice case of flu would give me more time to come up with something.

"Oh no, honey. Emmy left for California this morning. The car came to get her and take her to the airport real early. She's probably in L.A. by now."

Something deep in my chest slammed like a heavy wooden door, and a hollowness filled my belly. Somehow I had known it. "But... her flight's not till the day after tomorrow."

"Well, that's what we all thought, too, but that handsome young driver said, nope, today was the big day. Thank goodness Emmy was already packed." She laughed. "That girl's been packed for weeks—"

"How could everyone have gotten the date wrong?" I interrupted. "She didn't even say goodbye. And she's not answering her phone."

"Oh—she left her phone here. It was ringing earlier, but I don't really know how to answer those smart phone things. The young man said she'd be getting a brand new iPhone when she got there, anyway."

This was all too weird. Something was very wrong with the situation and with Emmy's mom, too. I'd never seen her act this spacey.

"So, someone came unexpectedly to pick Emmy up two days early and made her leave her phone at home?"

Mrs. Rooney laughed. "You should have seen her. She was so excited. I'd been kinda worried the past few months over the whole thing—California's so far away—but now I know she'll be fine. The man said there was nothing to worry about. Did I tell you how handsome he was? And so charming..." Her words drifted as her expression took on a dreamy glaze.

Dang it. She was glamoured. I'd never seen it up close and personal before. Not pretty.

"Mrs. Rooney, do you have Emmy's address in L.A.? Her new phone number?"

She looked at me, chin cocked to one side. I could almost see the question mark form in the air over her head.

"N-no. I guess I don't, but it will be fine because—"

"Yeah. I know. Because the handsome man said so. Okay, thanks Mrs. Rooney."

I trudged back to my car, my heart sinking. So that's how they did it, how they managed to "disappear" hundreds of young fans, inserting them into the fan pods of Dark Elven actors, musicians, politicians, and athletes without any sort of public outcry from worried family members. I guess if they saw them on Facebook smiling and posing at exciting Hollywood parties and premieres, Mom and Dad figured all was well. And of course they'd been assured everything would be "fine."

Emmy had explained the fan pod system to me in her car at the Sonic a few weeks ago when she'd first told me she'd applied for one. She'd mentioned an article in *People* magazine about some super-agent in Los Angeles who'd created the whole concept. I couldn't remember his name, but you'd better believe I broke a couple of rural speed limits to get back home to my laptop and look him up.

First I did a search on Vallon Foster and found his agent's name. Alfred Frey—that was it. There he was on Wikipedia.

Frey first became a fixture on the Hollywood scene in the early 90's and quickly rose to legendary status as the representative of an uncanny number of top movie and television stars as well as popular musical artists, professional athletes. Frey has even handled media relations for some of the country's top political figures and financial powerbrokers.

The entry went on to list the names of some celebrities Frey represented. I couldn't help but be impressed. The Dark Elves had been busy claiming the most prominent spots on the music charts, prime time television, the box office, and state and national political offices.

And the humans had no idea. They were hiding from us in plain sight. But why? What was their purpose in forming the fan pods and recruiting people like Emmy for them?

That's what Lad's father and the Light Elven High Council had wanted to find out during the Assemblage. I wondered if they'd gotten very far with the inquiry before Ivar was murdered. It had probably stopped immediately after his death. Was that *why* he was murdered?

Well, whatever they were up to, I knew what I had to do—find Emmy. And there was only one way to do it. I had to go to Los Angeles.

I was one of only a few, maybe even the *only* human who knew the truth about the fan pods. Without me, Emmy could end up like Allison Douglas, the girl from Deep River who'd gone out to L.A. to join a fan pod and come home in a casket.

I didn't know exactly how I'd go about finding her. Take one of those Hollywood tours of the stars' homes and jump out when we got to Vallon Foster's house? I wasn't sure. But it seemed talking to Grandma Neena was a good first step

"Well, you can't go alone, that's for certain," she said when I told her about my intentions. "You need help."

She gave me a hand rake, and I squatted down beside her among the baby summer squash in the garden to help remove the weeds. The scents of freshly turned earth and sun-warmed leaves settled my nerves but made me feel homesick, though I hadn't even left yet.

"There's no one to help me. Unless you want to come."

She sighed. "I'd love to, but it's been so long since I've been in touch with the Elven world, I'd most likely be useless to you. And someone has to stay here and get your tea company up and running on time. Someone who's able to communicate with the Elves and take delivery of the saol water to produce the tea. What about your friend Nox?"

The tines of my tool stabbed into the soft earth. "He's *not* my friend."

Shaking her head at my stubbornness, Grandma matched it with her own obstinate expression. "Well, I don't see what other choice you have. I won't allow you to go out there alone. Nox is sworn to protect you—"

I stood and brushed the dirt from my knees. "He's a Dark Elf. He was raised with Lad's family from the age of twelve, but he still might be on the Dark Elves' side. Besides, how much can his promises really mean? I don't trust him."

"Ryann." Standing to join me, Grandma shook her head sadly. "When did you become so suspicious of everything and everyone in the world?"

"I'm not suspicious of everyone. I trust you, and Mom, and Emmy, and Shalena."

"So, it's just the males of the species then?"

"Well, can you blame me? Daddy cheated on Mom and ran off and left us for almost a year. And Nox lied to me about who he was, and Lad—he's the worst of all—he told me he loved me and wanted to be with me forever, and then he ended it without a look back over his shoulder. So why exactly would I trust men?"

"Hello Maria," Grandma said loudly, no doubt a signal to me that any conversation about Elves should cease immediately. I hadn't heard Mom's approach.

I turned around to see an expression of deep concern on her face, the lines between her drawn eyebrows forming a small eleven. "Ryann... honey, I'm sorry for eavesdropping, but I overheard the last thing you said. We need to talk, sweetheart."

Great. The you-can-have-a-man-in-your-life-but-only-as-icing-on-the-cake-speech. She was preaching to the choir on that one now. "No we don't, Mom. You don't have to tell me anymore—you were right. You should never love someone more than he loves you, and you should never need anyone. It only leads to misery."

Her face fell into a sketch of sorrow and regret. She ran her hand through my hair, extracting part of a fuzzy squash leaf. "No, honey. That's not what I was going to say." She swallowed. "In fact, I was going to say the opposite. Poor kid—I've messed you up good, haven't I?"

I shrugged away from her touch, irritated. "I'm not messed up."

"I think I'll go see how the watermelons are coming along." Grandma turned to head for the far side of the garden.

Mom continued, a sympathetic softness in her voice. "Well, I've confused you, at least on the subject of love, right when you're at the stage of life when you should be opening your heart to it."

I shook my head in protest, but she continued. "I was wrong, Ryann. I was hurting, and at the time it seemed like good advice. But the truth is, I was miserable—filled with bitterness and distrust. I don't want that for you."

"Oh—and *now* you trust Daddy?" My tone was all sour sarcasm. In spite of the fact my father had returned and begged my forgiveness, begged Mom to take him back, they were not a couple again. While he was away, she'd started dating a man she'd met through mutual friends—a powerful Georgia senator, in fact. They were still seeing each other on a regular basis.

Her eyes grew even sadder. "Sweetie, there are so many things you don't know, and you *shouldn't* have to worry about all these adult problems. But I will tell you this— Daddy and I didn't break up over his infidelity."

I blinked, confused. A horsefly landed on my arm, and I brushed him away before he could sting me. "But you said..."

"I know. He did have a brief affair—but he did it to punish me, to make a point. I hurt him first, so I'm as much to blame for our problems as he is."

My head felt like a pinwheel spinning in a hurricane. I'd never heard this part of the story before. Why hadn't Dad said anything to defend himself? And what defense could there possibly *be*? "Mom—what did *you* do?"

Her gaze fell to the ground. She glanced over the rows of squash and peppers and tomatoes then back to me.

"We had a fight over the IRS thing. I was very angry, and I... said something I never should have said. Anyway..." She swished her hands in front of her chest like she could wipe away the unpleasantness of the past. "That's all behind us now."

Her expression and tone brightened. "And it *is* possible to find love again. Look at me and Davis. I've never felt this way about anyone—he's just—he's amazing, and I'm so happy. I know you're hurting right now, but you can believe me because I've *been* there. Your heart will heal, and you will find someone else to love—someone you'll love even more than Lad."

I stayed stock still, my gaze following a ladybug up a trellis where winding green bean vines intermingled and overlapped so thickly they'd never be pulled apart. She was wrong—I'd never love anyone more than I loved Lad. It was impossible.

And *she* was unbelievable. I wanted to run past the garden fence into the woods, screaming. After all of her preaching this past year about never needing a man, Mom was now telling me to trust in love.

Well, cynical as it was, her advice had been right the first time. I'd actually *defied* her icing-on-the-cake warning and given my whole heart to Lad—and look where that got me. I was alone and miserable, and he *wasn't* here when I needed him.

I do need him. The thought was arresting. I needed him—and for so much more than my own sake. He was the only answer to the Emmy situation.

Kicking a dirt clod with the toe of my shoe, I watched it roll into a garden stake and break in half. Lad might not want me anymore, but he would *have* to help me. He *knew* the Dark Elves were up to no good with the fan pods. He knew how much I cared about Emmy.

No matter what happened between us, he wouldn't just stand by while they hurt my friend. Besides, I had nowhere else to turn.

"Well, I'd better get back to work," I said to Mom.

Her sorrowful frown deepened as she backed up a couple steps and lifted a hand. "Okay, babe. I guess I'll go get dinner started and give Davis a call. He had a big committee meeting today in D.C. I'll tell him you said hi."

"Sure. You do that." I still hadn't met the *new* love of her life, and in my present mood, wasn't in any hurry to.

Chapter Four
Above It All

"I'm going to Altum," I announced after finding Grandma depositing some rotted tomatoes into the compost bin.

She looked up at me with wide eyes. "You can't. The High Council could decide to hold you there—indefinitely—on suspicion of involvement in Ivar's murder."

"Lad said he thinks I'm safe now—relatively safe. And I *have* to speak to him. He's the only one who can help me find Emmy and get her away from the fan pod. He'll help me—I know it—if I can just talk to him."

And if he agrees to help me, we'll be spending time together, and he'll remember he loves me, and... I tried to squelch the rising hope that this was the answer to finding Emmy and also to getting our relationship back on track.

Grandma didn't look so sure. "You can *ask*, honey, but I'm warning you—don't get your hopes up."

"So you won't try to stop me from going to him?"

She stepped away from the bin and brushed her dirt-covered hands together to clean them. "No, you're still to go nowhere near there. I'll go tomorrow and deliver a message asking him to meet you. You can wait at his tree nest."

"But if you go to Altum alone..." Was I selfishly putting her in danger?

She shushed me. "I'm immortal, remember? You're only part-Elven, so there's no guarantee *you* are. Don't you worry about your old grandma. Besides, the Council members already questioned me. They know I was with my family in their quarters at the time of the king's death, so I'm not a suspect."

We hiked through the familiar woods on her six hundred acre property. The air was extra muggy, though it was early morning, and the smell of hot pine needles permeated the atmosphere. Finally, we came to the huge tree where Lad and I first met as children.

I turned to ask Grandma one more time if I could go with her. "I think I could explain better how much I need him to help me."

"I'll get the message across, I promise. If Lad *can* come to you, he will. And if he *doesn't* come by noontime, you hightail it on home—with or without me. I don't want you out here alone for long."

I assured her I understood and watched as her wild white ringlets disappeared between the trees and brushy undergrowth. Climbing the large tree carefully, I made my way to the comfortable nest-like structure Lad had built as a child.

He'd continued to use it as a secret place where he could be alone and keep his most precious treasures. Like the library books he'd been forbidden to have. And the book I'd left behind when I was lost out here as a little girl. He'd used it to teach himself to understand our language.

Gradually, over many years, he'd become familiar with human life and culture through books and newspapers and magazines, making him an anomaly among the Light Elves, who held themselves completely apart from humans.

I pulled my old book out of the ancient chest that anchored the corner of the nest and looked through it then sifted through Lad's boyhood treasures. Arrowheads, feathers... a picture of me.

My heart contracted with a fierce beat. He must have taken it from the hall table the only time he'd ever been in my house, that day when he'd met Mom and Grandma Neena, the day Grandma realized he was the son of the Elven fiancé she'd jilted forty years ago—Lad's father, Ivar.

Hearing the scrabbling of feet on bark, I looked up to see Lad swing himself over the edge into the nest. He landed lightly on his toes and fingertips, crouching right in front of me.

Though it had been only a day since I'd last seen him, the vision of his beautiful face, his powerful body before me, shocked me with a jolt of pleasure that was almost violent. *How could I miss him so much already?*

"What are you doing here?" he snapped in an agitated tone. "I asked you not to come to me."

And there went all the good feelings. "*Sorry* to *bother* you." My tone sounded as hurt as I felt. Was he really completely over me, so fast, so easily?

He huffed an impatient breath. "What is it you need to say, Ryann? I don't have much time. I was in the middle of something."

Ouch. I'd hoped he might be at least a *tiny* bit pleased to see me, that maybe yesterday's conversation had been rooted in his pain and he'd had second thoughts about us.

Right. Well, hurt feelings or not, I still needed his help. I had to convince him.

"Fine—I'll try not to *waste* too much of your time. I'm here on business. Emmy has disappeared. A Dark Elf came to get her early to take her to her new fan pod, and I didn't have a chance to stop her from going. I don't have any contact information for her. Her family doesn't even know where she is, and they're not worried about her."

His eyes revealed a flicker of concern, but it didn't reach his voice. "Then maybe you shouldn't be."

"Are you serious?" I gasped. "You *know* I should be. You know what's going on with those fan pods."

He shook his head. "Not really. We don't know *what's* going on with them, only that they've been increasing rapidly in size and number recently. My father is… was concerned about them, but there's no *proof* there's any harm in them."

His nonchalant demeanor was ticking me off. Were the Light Elves really so above-it-all? And did my former "rebel" boyfriend suddenly think exactly like the rest of them? My blood pressure was rising along with the volume of my voice.

"No harm? They're going to glamour her brains out! Emmy will do and say whatever Vallon Foster tells her to, and she'll think she's happy about it. She won't be *Emmy* anymore. And what about what happened to that girl Allison Douglas? They did an autopsy, you know, and couldn't find any reason she died. She was nineteen years old, Lad. And my mom said the body looked totally normal when it arrived at the funeral home. Nineteen-year-old girls don't drop dead for no reason. They *did* something to her. Her family said the police out there aren't even investigating—I'm sure the detectives were glamoured, too."

He held up a hand to stop my rant, the expression on his face torn between regret and annoyance. "I'm sorry about your friend, Ryann—I am—but I can't do anything to help you."

"What?" I was having a hard time believing what I'd just heard. Did he not care at all? What happened to my sweet, open-minded, open-hearted boyfriend?

"I can't help you," he repeated, confirming that the Lad I'd known and loved had apparently died right along with his father.

"You mean you won't," my voice was choked with the threat of angry tears.

"I'm sorry. I can't leave Altum. I can't afford to give any of my time to this. Even if I could, I'm not sure how much help I could be to you. I had a very limited relationship with the Dark Elves before. And now since my father's—after he called off the wedding and what happened afterward—our relations with the Dark Elves are even more strained."

"Wait…" A new suspicion hit me like a poison-tipped arrow. "Do you blame *me* for what happened to your father? Do you think his murder was related to the cancelled wedding?"

He hesitated before answering, giving a long, slow blink. "I'm not sure what to think right now, Ryann. That's one reason I'm so busy—I'm trying to discover who's responsible for his death. But no, I don't blame you. I didn't want the marriage. I was only too happy to walk away from it when Father told me I could." He paused. "I have only myself to blame for that."

But if his father had been killed because of reneging on the marriage contract, at least some of the blame *had* to fall on me. I was the reason for it. If Lad had never met me, he probably would have been happy to marry a beautiful Elven girl of royal blood, even if she was the daughter of the Dark Elves' leader. The union had made political sense to all of them, and in the brief moments I saw her, she certainly seemed to be in favor of it.

"Have you spoken to Vancia since then?" I asked in a small voice.

Lad's entire body went still. His eyes softened for a moment as he fixed them on mine. And then they turned back to glistening green stone and held something that looked a lot like pity.

He stood, obviously preparing to leave. "I have to go back, Ryann. I don't have time to deal with your... insecurities and jealousy. I know your concern about your friend seems like a very big thing to you right now, but I'm sure she'll be fine." His lips rolled in to form a tight line. "Don't send me any more messages. It's hard on both of us to meet like this, and... I won't come next time. So please, just—don't."

He disappeared over the edge of the nest, leaving me standing with my jaw hanging open and my heart in tatters. Insecurities. Jealousy. *What a jerk.*

I'd been too stunned to interrupt, and he'd given me no chance to reply, but his callous words now played through my mind in a continuous loop. *I know your concern about your friend seems like a very big thing to you.*

Furious tears erupted and ran down my face. If he'd wanted to ensure I never came looking for him again, he'd succeeded brilliantly. Who *was* this guy? Certainly not the Lad I'd fallen in love with, the sweet, sensitive boy who'd been my hero in so many ways. Now he was truly his father's son.

I trudged home, alternating between states of fury and despair. There was no part of me that wanted to go out tonight. Shay and I had planned to take Emmy out in Oxford for a last hurrah, but of course that wasn't happening now.

When I called to give her the news about Emmy's early departure, Shay didn't seem all that surprised or worried. And she still wanted to get together. I finally agreed to cruise the Sonic and the ballpark with her for a while. She was hoping her new crush Lance would be around. And maybe seeing her would help—I might pick up a clue or two that would lead me to Emmy.

She had certainly been more receptive to hearing about Emmy's big plans these past few weeks, so she very well might have more information about them than I did. Maybe Emmy had even mentioned something to Shay about where she'd be staying in L.A. or how to reach her.

I took Grandma's car into town and pulled up to Shay's house, a gingerbread Victorian that had to be at least a hundred years old, like the rest of the houses on her street. She must have been watching from the window because she came out the front door, crossed the porch, and ran down the steps to where I'd parked on the street.

Opening the passenger door, she slid into the seat in a whoosh of energy and Viva La Juicy perfume. "Hey girl!"

"Hey. You look cute," I said. She did look adorable, as her pageant-girl self always did. She was only saved from universal female hatred by her consistent niceness. You just couldn't not like her.

"You, too," she said. "Hey, what's the matter? You seem bummed."

I started the car and began the short drive to Sonic. "I'm fine. I'm... I'm worried about Emmy, I guess."

"Well stop worrying—she's partying her ass off in La La Land right now. I'm sure she'll call us this weekend when she gets settled."

"So... you don't have a number for her? Or an address?" I glanced over at her in the passenger seat.

"No. Do you?"

My shoulders sagged as the hope leached from my body. "No. I have no idea how to reach her."

"Well, she just got there—give her time. Anyway, we can ask her mom."

"Yeah." I sighed, already aware of how useless that tactic was.

When I turned the car into Sonic, Shay sat up straight in her seat and practically wiggled with excitement. "There's Lance with his friends. You wanna get out and talk to them?"

"No, you go ahead. I'll stay in the car."

"You sure?"

I pulled into one of the diagonal parking spaces. "Yeah. I want to order something."

Actually, I wanted to just get through the evening. My last hope for information about Emmy's whereabouts was gone—Shay knew nothing. I already knew Emmy's parents were clueless. Lad wasn't going to be any help. I was completely on my own.

I couldn't even begin to solve the problem tonight, though. I had plans to drown my sorrows in microwave popcorn and a Vampire Diaries marathon as soon as Shay got her Lance fix and said we could leave.

A knock at my window startled me, causing me to jump. On the other side of it, Nox stood smiling and gesturing for me to roll the window down. I glanced through the windshield at Shay, who was in full-flirt with Lance, leaning against the hood of his car. *Dang it.* I couldn't just drive off and leave her.

Heaving a heavy sigh, I rolled the window down. "What are you doing here? I thought you had gone out to L.A. with your band to get ready for a world tour or something."

"And it's *nice* to see you, too." His voice danced with sarcasm. "I'll be heading there soon. I'm taking a short break from world domination at the moment."

When his wit failed to elicit a smile from me, Nox got serious. He rested his forearms on the top of the window frame, putting his face much too close to mine as he bent and sort of hung into the car. "Listen, I heard about your friend Emmy. I'm sorry."

"Sure you are." I looked away and fiddled with the stereo controls.

"No really, I'm sorry. You're upset. And believe it or not, whatever bothers you bothers me."

I shrugged. "Well, thanks I guess, but apparently there's nothing anyone can do."

"What do you mean?"

"I mean, I don't even know how to begin to find her short of going to Los Angeles and driving around hoping to spot her walking down Sunset Boulevard. I've already tried to get some help, and... well, that's not happening."

"You mean the police?"

I shot him a give-me-a-break glance. "You know they can't do anything. No. I mean I asked Lad to help me."

His dark eyebrows lifted. "He turned you down?"

"Never mind. I'll figure it out." I pressed the button to raise the car window, causing him to back away from the opening.

He grabbed the top of the window glass before it closed completely. "Wait. Wait. Maybe I can help. I do have some connections in California. As you said, I've been out there a lot these past few months, rehearsing and getting things ready for the tour."

"No," I blurted. Connections or not, I didn't trust Nox. Not anymore. He hadn't been honest with me and had very possibly glamoured me with his music for purposes only he knew. No way was I going to put my faith in him. I was better off alone.

Shay picked that moment to walk back to the car. *Thank God.* Now we could leave, and I could get away from Nox and home to the beautiful Salvatore brothers. *Shoot*—were they Elven, too? Probably.

"Hi Nox. Hey Ryann, would you mind if I ride around with Lance for a while?" Shay gave me a big grin that told me their conversation had gone *very well*. Their "ride" would probably end up out at the end of the not-quite-finished bypass where kids took their cars to park and hook up.

I blew out a breath and forced a smile. Someone in this godforsaken town should be happy. "Sure. That's great. So, he'll take you home later then?"

She nodded, still wearing the giddy grin, and I gave her a thumbs-up. "Goodbye Nox," I said, closing the window completely and putting the car into reverse.

He stood for a moment, too close to allow me to back out of my parking spot without crushing his toes, but then he fell back a few steps, and I pulled out and drove away, not bothering to look into the rearview mirror.

CHAPTER FIVE
DEAL WITH THE DEVIL

My mom shook me awake early the next morning.

"What's going on?" I mumbled. "It's Saturday—I mean it's summer." I rolled to face her and forced my heavy eyelids open.

"Nox is here," she whispered. "Do you want to see him, or should I tell him to come back later?"

I sat up in bed, instantly awake. What the heck was he doing here? "No, I'll get up. Give me a minute."

It would have done me no good to try to go back to sleep, knowing Nox was right on the other side of my bedroom door. *What does he want?* And what was he doing *in my house?*

"Well, I'm on my way to work in a minute, but Grandma is here." She kissed my forehead and hugged my shoulders. "Have a good day, okay? I'll see you tonight."

Giving her a smile and a wave, I slid out of bed. I'd brush my teeth and throw on some shorts and a t-shirt, then get rid of Nox as quickly as possible.

The last thing I needed was him hanging around and glamouring Mom into whatever whim he had on his mind. She might be on her way out, but it was no secret she always had a few minutes to spare for him. Like most other females, she was highly susceptible to his charms, in spite of her half-Elven heritage.

Glancing at the mirror, I momentarily considered trying to deal with the bed head but decided it really didn't matter. Maybe the Medusa look would scare him away.

I walked into the great room to find Nox's huge form taking up half the sofa. He stood when he saw me and looked me over, his gaze landing on my hot pink toenails before traveling up to my cosmetic-free face. His smile was wide and thoroughly irritating.

"Good morning." His voice carried a note of amusement. "You look like a little girl without your makeup on."

My face heated, making up for the lack of foundation and blusher. "What do you want, Nox?"

"I guess I can't get enough of your friendly face and charming personality lately," he said, laughing softly at my less-than-amused expression. "Fine. I'm here because I have something *you* want."

"Right. I don't think so."

"You want to find Emmy. I can help you do that."

"How can you help me? She's in L.A. in a fan pod. What—you have some kind of fan pod directory?"

"No—but I do have a fan pod. Or... I *can* have one." His brow lifted in a *so-there* way.

I froze in place. "What do you mean?"

"My agent is Alfred Frey. He's been bugging me about starting a pod for months now, and I've been putting him off. But maybe this is the right time. If I move out to L.A. full-time and let him set one up for me, I might be able to get some insider information. You could come with me, and we could find Emmy—together."

Dumbfounded, I looked at him for a few moments, trying to get it through my head that Nox, who I'd known for months, who I'd thought I'd known so well, *really was* a Dark Elf. I mean, I knew it in theory—I'd discovered that fact on the day of Lad's cancelled wedding, the day Lad's father was found murdered. But, it was so hard to believe.

And now... with this revelation, that he had a fan pod just waiting to be born, I had a whole new level of disbelief to process. Nox was a celebrity. A fledgling celebrity, but big enough to have a fan pod of his own, like Vallon Foster the movie star, and Serena Simmons the supermodel-turned-actress, and Reggie Dillon the NFL quarterback, and countless other famous athletes and performers who seemed too good to be true.

As it turned out, they all were.

At my silence he continued. "So, you know The Hidden has been working on our album in the studio, and we're getting ready to go out on tour this fall? I've been flying back and forth to L.A. so much I was already thinking of moving into my house there full-time. The band's got a lot of pre-tour promotion we have to do anyway—TV and radio station appearances. I haven't actually met Vallon yet, but once I move out there, it probably wouldn't be too hard to meet up with him."

"Wait. Slow down. You have a *house* in Los Angeles?"

"Yep. Right on the beach in Malibu. It could be home base for Operation Find Emmy. Sound like a plan?"

When Nox had mentioned being out in California lately, I certainly never imagined he already had a house there, much less a beach house in Malibu. And the idea of going there *with* him—it did sound like a plan. A dangerous one.

"I... don't think so."

Nox rested his hands on his hips and threw back his head as if the answer to persuading me was written across the ceiling. His voice was rough with exasperation. "Ahhh... Ryann. Come *on*. This is what you wanted, right? A way to find Emmy? You're not going to get a better offer."

That much was true. I wasn't going to get *any* other offers at all. But traveling with Nox—

Blinking in rapid succession, I blew out a breath. "I don't know. I need to think. And I can't think with you standing right there, pressuring me."

A confident smile overtook his face. "Fine. You think about it." He walked toward the door as he talked, throwing a grin back over his shoulder. "Then let me know what day I should book the plane tickets."

Before he reached the door, Grandma came into the room from the kitchen. She and Nox stared into each other's eyes for a few moments, and he left, laughing as the door clicked shut behind him.

"What do you think, Grandma?" We sat at the breakfast table together where I'd shared Nox's plan with her.

"I'm not sure. I told you before he was probably your only hope. But even if he has the best intentions, Nox doesn't seem to understand any more about what the Dark Elves are up to than we do. A few minutes ago when I suggested they might have nefarious purposes, he laughed."

"Well, he's been with the Light Elves since he was a child. He's only just started associating with the Dark Elves again—maybe he doesn't know anything. Or... maybe he's lying."

"No. He's not lying. Whatever's going on with the fan pods, he really means to look out for you out there and bring you home safely. It's impossible for us to lie when we communicate in the Elven way, mind-to-mind."

"Oh, wow." That was a revelation. I really needed to work on developing my Elven communication skills. I'd love to know what was *really* going on inside that inflated head of his. Of course, Nox was plenty capable of deceiving without actually telling any lies.

I'd known him almost a year, and he'd never told me a direct lie—yet he'd managed to keep me from finding out he was Elven. And Lad's foster brother. Nox was a master of omission.

Even if I became an expert in Elven communication, I'd still only be able to hear the thoughts he *wanted* me to hear—those he sent to me. Elves didn't walk around reading everything in each other's minds. If Nox had anything to hide, I had no doubt he'd still manage to keep it from me.

How could I trust him?

How could I find Emmy *without* him?

Both questions had the same answer.

I couldn't.

"I don't think I have a choice. If it were me who'd disappeared off the face of the earth, and I had a friend who might be able to help, wouldn't you want her to? Wouldn't you do it for your friend, for your sister?"

Grandma Neena had only recently been reunited with her own sister, even her parents, after a forty-year estrangement. She'd been happier about that than I'd seen her in my whole life.

"I don't have a sister, but Emmy's the closest thing I've got," I continued. "And there may literally be no other human on the planet who can help her."

Her hands lifted then fell onto the tabletop. "Well, I guess it's decided then. What will you tell your momma?

How will you explain your sudden desire to fly out to L.A.?"

"She knows I've always been fascinated with UCLA. I'll say I want to visit the campus. She respects education and career-readiness more than anything. You know that. And I'll use my waitressing money for the ticket. If she still doesn't go for it, I know someone who can glamour her— quite easily, in fact."

"Yes, that's true." She chuckled, understanding my reference to Nox. Then all amusement left her face. She took my hands and looked into my eyes. "I'm worried about this Ryann. I'll cover for you and work to get the tea company going here while you're gone, but you have to promise me something."

Her seriousness alarmed me. "What?"

"Promise me when you look for Emmy you'll *look*, only—not confront anyone, not try to perform some cockamamie rescue operation by yourself. Let Nox deal with the Dark Elves—you're not up to the task. They're not like me and Lad."

I nodded as she went on, her fingers tightening around mine until it was almost painful.

"And I need to hear from you often—the *truth* about what's going on. If I find out *you've* joined a fan pod… I'll be getting on a plane myself."

"Don't worry, Grandma." I patted her hand in reassurance. "That will never happen."

CHAPTER SIX
UP, UP AND AWAY

The flight attendant handed me a bubbling, icy Coke and gave Nox the beer he'd asked for, lingering to make sure there was nothing *else* he needed before moving on to serve the other first class passengers.

"You should have some of this. It'll help with those first-time jitters," he said, holding out the foam-topped glass to me.

Nox had insisted on buying our tickets—thus the first class seating. My money would probably have gotten me a lovely seat conveniently located right outside the plane's rear lavatory, but I suspected I still would have been more comfortable there. He looked entirely comfortable with the relative luxury, already reclining and enjoying his pre-flight beverage.

I shook my head. "I don't have jitters about flying."

"You have jitters about *something*." Cutting a side glance at me, he picked up a Luxury Pools magazine someone had left behind. He flipped through the pages wearing a smug smile.

I pulled at the end of my seatbelt strap again—still fastened—before folding my hands in my lap and focusing my attention out the window. Within minutes we were backing out of the gate, taxiing down the runway, and lifting off for my first trip to California and my first stretch of enforced togetherness with Nox since discovering the truth about him.

I pretended to sleep for most of the flight. Real sleep proved impossible. My mind was too active, filled with equal parts anticipation and apprehension about what would be waiting for us when we touched down.

Some things I'd expected, like the bright sunshine outside the window as we taxied to the terminal and disembarked, and the massive crowd inside. And there were people actually holding up those little signs for arriving passengers like they did in the movies—I wasn't sure if that was a real thing before now.

Of course, there wasn't a sign for us—we didn't need one. Only one of the waiting drivers looked like a professional volleyball player or a male model. Or both. He nodded to Nox as we approached him, and we followed our ridiculously handsome chauffeur outside to the curb where a gleaming black Hummer waited. He opened the back door for us.

"You have to be kidding me," I said to Nox as I climbed in. "Who lives like this?"

He gave me a dazzling grin as he slid into the seat beside me. "Welcome to L.A., Ryann. You're going to like it in my world."

Palm trees. I was getting butterflies looking at palm trees outside of the tinted windows, and we hadn't even left the airport yet. *What a country bumpkin.* Glancing over at Nox, I did a double take at his expression. He'd been watching me stare out the window as we rode in silence, and he looked completely amused at my wide-eyed wonder.

"Shut up," I said and turned back to the window, propping my head on my hand.

He laughed and started singing, "I… know a place… where the grass is really greener. Warm… wet and wild—"

I clamped my hands over my ears. "Stop. Stop it. Do *not* sing to me—about California or anything else."

"Come on, Ryann. You like it." He snickered, a rascally sound. "And you're so much more fun when you're a little bit glamoured."

I sucked in a breath and snapped my attention to him before turning my head away again, face burning. So he *knew* what his singing did to me. Of course. I should've known he'd figure out the real reason I'd never gone back to see him perform after the first time in Oxford.

One song, and I'd been ready to start a fan pod for him and nominate myself as its president. His voice was… indescribable. Dangerous. The heat spread from my face to my neck as I realized why he'd hummed on the two occasions he'd kissed me. And why it had taken everything in me to resist him. I folded my arms tightly over my chest and continued staring out the window.

In my peripheral vision, Nox took out his phone and tapped the screen.

"It's me. I'll be coming in this afternoon. Yes. Right. Hold on." He pressed the phone to his chest and leaned in my direction. "Would you like Aiden to drive around a bit, give you a tour of the Hollywood hotspots? See the Walk of Fame? Rodeo Drive? Mann's?"

"No." My voice was brittle. "We're here to find Emmy. Nothing else."

Grinning, Nox put the phone back to his ear. "We'll be there within the hour. Right. Good." He hung up and answered my unspoken question. "Notifying my staff to expect us. They'll have some supper ready."

Shock pulled me around to face him. "You have a *staff*?"

Nox's grin widened. "Listen Ryann, I know we're here to find Emmy, but you might as well loosen up and enjoy the fringe benefits of the situation—do some sight-seeing while you're here, try to have some fun. We can't exactly drive up to Vallon Foster's mansion, ring the doorbell, and demand he turn her over. We'll have to be a *little* more subtle than that. It's going to take some time."

I narrowed my gaze at him. "What does that mean?"

"It means he can't suspect what we're up to, or all Hell's gonna break loose. *No one* can find out you know

58

our secret. Which they *will* if you go marching up to his front gate pushing the buzzer and screaming "Emmy!" in the streets of Brentwood. It's gonna look pretty strange if even *I* start asking questions or make it obvious I'm looking for her."

"So—what then? You tell your agent you're here, let him recruit some stupid groupies for your new fan pod, and then we all have a groupie play date? You bring your pets, he brings his?"

Nox laughed. "Something like that."

"And how will you explain me? If you have a staff, other Elves are obviously going to find out I'm here with you."

"True." He paused a moment, a here-comes-the-punch-line expression on his face. "Looks like I have the first official member of my fan pod."

Silence filled the car, expanding like an oversized helium balloon.

No doubt sensing my displeasure, Nox tried to placate me. "Only as far as everyone else knows. I mean, you'd only be pretending. All you have to do is spend a little time with me, go to a few parties, act like you don't hate me—"

"I'm not that good of an actress." I tried playing the hard-ass, but as I'd just confessed, I wasn't a good actress. "Oh all right. I guess there's no other way to do this. But don't expect a lot of giggling and squee-ing."

"No, of course not." Nox tried to hold a sober expression, but an amused grin broke through as he turned his head toward his own window and checked out the view of the freeway. After a few seconds his shoulders shook with his silent laughter.

"What?" My tone revealed every ounce of my annoyance. "What?"

He finally laughed out loud. "I can't picture it. I bet you've never 'squee-ed' once in your entire life."

His laughter was so contagious, I had to join him. "I did. Once." I shrugged and nodded. "Justin Beiber. I was eleven."

"Figures." He snorted.

"Why?"

"He's *not* Elven."

CHAPTER SEVEN
DEALBREAKER

I woke to sunshine streaming in through floor-to-ceiling windows, momentarily confused by the sound of the Pacific surf. Someone had come in while I was sleeping and opened the French doors between my room and the balcony.

I'd vacationed at the beach before—my family used to drive down to Destin, Florida, at least once a year and rent an oceanside hotel room. This was a whole different category of oceanside room, one of many in Nox's house.

I'd been furious last night when Nox refused to instruct the driver to take me to a hotel. He'd insisted on my spending the night at his home. To do otherwise would raise suspicion, he said.

After dropping that bomb on me, Nox immediately lowered the privacy window between the front and back seats of the Hummer and put his finger to his lips. "Servants talk," he scribbled on the side of his boarding pass envelope.

I'd shoved the paper back at him and given him a dirty look, the only thing I could do, since protesting out loud would have revealed to the driver that I was neither a legitimate fan pod member nor under his glamour. The ruse had begun.

And now I was waking up in Nox's house, in his bed. Well, not *his* bed—a bed that belonged to him. It was large and ridiculously luxurious, like the rest of the Spanish-styled mansion. I got up and padded across the floor toward the open doors. How could I resist the lure of that view, the blue water stretching out to forever?

The stone tile was wonderfully warm under my bare feet, and the California morning sunshine did not fail to live up to its reputation. I leaned out over the railing to check out the beach below. A lone jogger passed, disturbing a trio of seagulls who were intent on finding their breakfast. The whole scene was so peaceful, so pleasing, I had to remind myself I wasn't happy to be here. I wasn't here to enjoy the scenery.

But someone else apparently was. When I turned to walk back into my room, I stopped short at the sight of Nox standing in the doorway, his long arms stretched out to either side, hands propped on the frame.

"You're awake." He eyed my t-shirt clad figure and bare legs with a raised brow and an appreciative nod.

"Yes, and *you're* in *my* room."

"I brought breakfast." Nox stepped back and made an inviting gesture with his arm.

I walked past him, pulling the hem of my sleep-tee down further over the tops of my thighs, and stopped at the small bistro table where a lavish breakfast had been set up.

"You said you had a staff for this kind of thing."

"Yes, well, they cooked it actually. But I didn't want to overwork them on our first day here. I thought I'd help by bringing it up. Sit down—you must be starving. I was told you didn't eat anything last night."

When I'd been unable to convince Nox to let me sleep elsewhere and he'd brought me here last night, I'd asked to see my room and then walked inside and shut the door, leaving him in the hallway alone. After attempting to talk to me through the door and receiving nothing but silence on my end, he finally gave up.

I'd showered in the huge, beautiful attached bathroom and gone right to bed, physically and mentally exhausted.

But now I was famished. Faced with the display of delicious-smelling food, my stomach reminded me of that skipped supper. I sat down at the table and picked up a fork.

"Well?" I looked up at Nox.

"What?"

"Are you going to stand there and watch me eat, because if you are, that's pretty weird."

"So, this is okay for you? I mean, it looks good?"

Why was he so concerned about my breakfast enjoyment? "It's fine. It's food. It'll do. *What* is your deal?"

"I want you to be comfortable here. If this food isn't to your liking, you can send it back and ask for something else. Whatever you want—ask for it and it's yours."

"You know what I want, Nox," I growled, stabbing at the scrambled eggs on my plate. "Just get me to Emmy, and I'll take her home and get out of your hair, the sooner the better."

He pulled out the other chair and sat down opposite me at the table. His tone was quiet and cautious. "I told you—it's going to take some time. And until we find her…" He took a deep breath. "…you're going to have to live here."

My fork clattered against the plate as I dropped it. "What?"

"As a member of my fan pod, you'll have to live here. That's how it's done."

"You mean—all those celebrities with fan pods—the members all *live* in their houses? At their beck and call day and night?"

Now he blushed. "Something like that. In ancient days when Elves ruled over humans, that was how it was. The Dark Elves are trying to restore the old system, I guess. I don't know much about it—only what Alfred has told me, which isn't much."

"Well if you think I'm going to live here and be part of your… *harem*, you're wrong." I shoved back from the table. Leaving my full plate, I marched across the room to where I'd dropped my clothes on the floor the night before and grabbed the pile, heading for the bathroom. "And why am I just now learning about this little detail? I'll find Emmy myself. Thanks for breakfast." The bathroom door slammed behind me with a satisfying bang.

When I'd showered and dressed, I went downstairs, suitcase in hand, to meet the taxi I'd called.

Nox was waiting for me on the bottom step. He held my arm as I attempted to pass him. "Please don't leave, Ryann. You need my help." His voice was low and urgent.

Having no other choice, I stopped. With him standing one step below me, we were eye-to-eye. I didn't like looking directly into that inhumanly beautiful hazel gaze, but I made myself do it.

"Maybe, maybe not," I lifted my chin. "But I don't need *anything* enough to trade my—"

Leaning close to my ear, he whispered, "I *know* that. I'd never expect you to—" He broke off with a frustrated sound. "We have to put on a good show for the staff and for Alfred—make them think I have a real fan pod and you're a member. I would never try to take advantage of the situation."

I pulled back and leveled an incredulous look at him. "Oh no. Not *you*," I said, sarcasm dripping from the words. "It's not like you've already tried to take advantage of me, is it? Like when you tried to seduce me and *pretended* to care about me."

Nox's brows pulled together in an angry slant. "I was not pretending."

"And *I* wasn't seduced," I countered, jerking my arm away and pushing past him.

Following me to the door, he let out an exasperated breath. "Look, I know I'm not the one you want. You've made that very clear. But I *am* the one who's here. And I do care about you—I want to help you. If you'll let me. Please don't leave."

The desperation in his tone took some of the wind out of my sails, but it didn't change the fact that being so far from home and living in his house put me in way too vulnerable a position. Glancing back to him with my hand on the door pull, I said, "You already have helped me. You got me here. Now I'll do the rest. Thanks for the plane ticket—I'm going to pay you back—I'll send the money when I get home—*with* Emmy. Good luck with your tour preparations."

I opened the door and hurried toward the taxi waiting at the curb outside the gates of the estate. As it drove away, my gaze was pulled back to the mansion. Nox was standing in the front doorway, watching me go.

Turning my head, I let the view through the windshield replace the image but couldn't block out the mental picture of his sad eyes, their blended color looking more green than brown as he'd pleaded with me not to leave him.

CHAPTER EIGHT
FAIL

Vallon Foster's house was on the Map of the Stars' Homes after all. According to the cab driver, Vallon lived in a mansion formerly owned by one of the biggest action movie stars of the past few decades.

For a moment I wondered if that guy had been an Elf, too—he did look super-young for his age—but then I read he'd recently gotten divorced from his wife, and his hair hadn't turned white. Or maybe it *had* and he'd died it to cover the mark. Then again, he *was* a Dark Elf. They were different from the Light Elves—in so many ways. Maybe they could fool around with as many people as they wanted to without consequence.

In any case, I'd found the house and hopefully found Emmy as well. All I had to do now was get inside. I paid the cabbie, adding a few dollars for a tip.

"Good luck," he said. His tone made the encouraging remark sound more like "fat chance."

Stepping onto the sidewalk, I surveyed the high ivy-covered walls surrounding the estate. The house must have been set far back from the road because it wasn't even visible. There was an iron gate across the drive and beside it, an intercom box I assumed would connect me with some sort of security person. It seemed like my best bet, short of scaling the walls and possibly finding some unhappy Dobermans on the other side.

Pushing the button, I waited for a response. A quiet whirring noise caused me to turn my head to the side where a video camera panned around and then focused on me. Okay, so they could see I wasn't an armed robber now. They could also see I wasn't a maid or serviceperson.

Could I pretend to be one of Vallon's stray fan pod members who'd gotten lost? Did someone keep up with them all—remember all their names and faces? Emmy had told me he had at least two hundred members in his fan pod at a time. Maybe they'd buy the "little lost sheep" act.

"Yes?" asked a feminine voice.

I leaned toward the box, angling my mouth at what looked like the receiver. "Hi. Um… I got left behind when we went… out. Can I come in?"

"State your name."

Dang. It wasn't going to work. They did keep some kind of records of their members. And I didn't dare say my real name. What was the most common name I knew? "Taylor?"

There was a pause. Then the voice came back, sounding sterner this time. "All of our Taylors are accounted for. If you would like to see Mr. Foster, he has a movie premier at the end of this month and will be walking the red carpet. Check his website if you'd like to apply for his fan pod. And please do not attempt to access his personal estate again. All trespassers will be immediately apprehended and turned over to the authorities. Goodbye." The monitor fell silent.

Well, that was super. I turned around and sat on the curb. *What the heck do I think I'm doing? I'm not Veronica Mars.* I didn't know the first thing about investigating or finding missing persons… or breaking and entering. Unless I happened to catch Emmy at the movie premier, there was no way to get close to her. Not without help.

Not without Nox.

When I pushed the buzzer at Nox's gate that night, the reception was entirely different. It immediately clicked and swung wide, and a man's voice said, "Please come in, Miss Carroll," through the speaker.

I had barely set foot on the driveway when the front door burst open. Nox rushed out to meet me. "Are you all right? Did something happen?" Worried eyes catalogued me from sunburned face to tired toes.

I sighed as he took my suitcase, relieving my aching arms. "I'm fine. And no—absolutely nothing happened. I didn't see a soul. I couldn't even get inside the gate." Sighing again, I prepared to humble myself and admit defeat. "Go ahead and say you told me so."

Assured of my well-being, Nox's face relaxed. "I'm sorry you had no luck. I was afraid that's what would happen. Based on the security they've provided for me here, I'm not surprised the Dark Council would have Vallon well-protected."

Leading me into the house, he peppered me with questions. "Are you hungry? Would you like to have a meal sent to your room? Or... I was eating on the patio when you rang the buzzer—you could join me if you like."

I was starving. And hot. And tired. Sitting out in the ocean breeze listening to the waves sounded too good to resist. "Yes. That would be nice."

His face brightened. "Good. It's this way."

I followed Nox through the enormous house to a set of French doors that opened up to a gorgeous pool deck and a stone lanai running the entire width of the house. The sun had almost set, but there was still a faint light visible over the horizon, giving the ocean a glowing border that appeared to be made of smoldering coals.

As we stepped out onto the lanai, a servant was leaving, having placed another platter of food as well as a new plate and set of silverware on the table.

I darted my eyes at Nox. "Oh. So you told her..."

He nodded. "She was near the kitchen when we passed through. I told her I would have a dinner companion after all."

"She's Elven then?"

"Yes. Most of the staff are."

He pulled out a chair for me and waited as I took my seat, then took his own. "I hope you like seafood. It's all fresh-caught—there's an assortment there for you to choose from." Lifting the lid of the platter, he gestured to the variety of fish and shellfish his chef had prepared. There was far more there than two people could ever eat. Dark Elves apparently liked to live well.

The scent of the grilled fish and savory vegetables wafted up, filling my nose and making my mouth spike with saliva. I was ravenous. Thirsty, too.

"Any sweet tea?"

That got a big smile out of him. "I'm afraid my staff isn't used to providing that particular beverage. Maybe you could make some for us while you're here—we do have saol water on hand."

I smiled back. "Maybe I will, and if you're *really* nice, maybe I'll share."

I had brought some saol water with me, in the metallic flask Lad had given me a few weeks ago, during better times. A tiny amount went a long way, but it was nice to know there was more in case I did actually want to whip up my special recipe sweet tea. Then again maybe not—the thought of cooking in Nox's kitchen was too strange.

I lifted a portion of fish onto my plate along with some salad. "So, you were eating alone then? I guess your fan pod hasn't arrived yet."

My tone was snarky, but Nox didn't seem bothered. He seemed... resigned. "Well, actually, quite a few members did arrive this afternoon. Alfred was *very* enthusiastic when I told him I'd finally agree to having one. There was already a wait list apparently."

"Oh. And you didn't want to eat with them?" I took a bite of fish. It was buttery and delicious. Kudos to the chef.

"Definitely not. I haven't even met them yet. It feels weird to have a bunch of strangers in my house, though I guess I'll have to see them eventually." He put his fork down and caught my gaze in his. "I'm so glad you came back... I was worried about you."

Feeling suddenly shy for some reason, I returned my attention to my plate. "The streets of Brentwood aren't exactly dangerous territory."

"You never know. If they turned you away immediately, why were you gone for so long? What did you do all day?"

I shrugged. "Walked around Vallon's neighborhood, looking at the houses—at high walls and gates mostly—people sure like their privacy out here. Then I walked into the village at Brentwood, sat at Starbucks all afternoon, trying to figure out what to do next." I looked down at my plate, stirring the food around with my fork. "I was embarrassed to come back here, to admit I needed help. And after the way I acted... I wasn't sure you'd let me in."

His hand reached out to cover mine. "I'm happy you're back. And… I'm happy to be needed. That doesn't happen very often."

The odd remark drew my eyes back to his, but I quickly looked down again. Pulling my hand from beneath his, I used it to readjust the napkin in my lap, though it had been draped perfectly fine already.

"You're a star. Everyone wants to be around you. I've seen it."

"They think they want me. But they don't even know me," he argued. "And no one *needs* me. There's a difference. When my parents died, I was lucky to have my aunt and uncle to take me in… but I never really *belonged* there at Altum. I always felt different. While they were kind to me, I always felt like they were *stuck* with me, you know? I had no real role there. Lad always knew he would grow up and be king. He knew exactly what was expected of him. I had no real purpose. It didn't really matter what I did. All of Ivar's attention was reserved for Lad—he was obsessed with making him the perfect future ruler. I gave up trying to please Ivar and actually *tried* to make him angry with me, make him punish me. I broke rules—even came home once wearing human clothes, expecting him to be furious. He barely noticed." Nox's tone turned morose. "They didn't even miss me when I turned sixteen and began staying away for longer and longer periods of time, playing with the band, traveling."

"I'm sure that's not true. Lad told me they did wonder where you were—and *he* missed you, at least."

He huffed a humorless laugh. "Well... I'm sure he's gotten over *that*."

"So... you two had a falling out then. Over me?" The thought of Lad feeling passionate enough about me to be angry with Nox made me happy and depressed at the same time. A renewed sense of loss swamped me and made me even more tired than I was already.

Nox leaned back in his chair and surveyed the rolling waves and the nearly dark sky above them. "Oh yes. He was... *not pleased* with me when he found out I'd been spending time with you. After he saw us together in your yard—the day he was shot—I was almost afraid to ever go home again. Really, I didn't go back until the Assemblage. I figured it would be safe then with all those visiting witnesses around. And of course, since he was getting married, there wasn't much he could say to me anymore on the subject. I had hoped we might bury the hatchet that day."

I winced at the memory of the heartbreaking visit to Lad's home, discovering it was his wedding day, running into Nox there in his full Elven garb.

"Why didn't you tell me?" He could have no doubt about what my quiet question referred to.

Turning back to me, his eyes pleaded for understanding. "You know why. Keeping the secret of our existence is our most sacred law. It's hammered into us from the earliest age. To have broken it would have meant danger for you and probably eternal banishment for me."

"But now I know. And instead of banishing you, Lad left me with you, told you to take care of me. Why? It doesn't make sense. Why would he choose you?"

Nox's intense gaze revealed the answer before his words did. "Because he knew I would. He knew I'd do *anything* for you."

For a moment, the two of us held blazing eye contact. I was having difficulty finding my breath.

Suddenly uncomfortable, I pushed away from the table and stood, knocking my water glass over in the process. "Oh, my gosh—I'm so sorry."

Nox jumped from his seat and lifted his plate to remove it from the pathway of the approaching tabletop flood. As soon as he picked up the dishware, the breeze caught a piece of paper that had been tucked underneath and blew it across the table toward me. Instinctively, I grabbed it to keep it from blowing off the patio onto the beach.

I barely had my fingers on it before Nox snatched the paper from my hands. "Thanks. I've got it," he said in a breathless rush.

"What is it? A letter?"

I couldn't see it well, but there appeared to be several paragraphs of handwriting on the page.

An uncharacteristic blush colored his face in the light of the deck lamps. He folded the paper several times and stuffed it into the pocket of his shorts. "It's nothing. Just a new song I'm working on."

"Let me see it," I ordered sweetly.

The blush deepened. *Interesting.*

"Nah—it's not very good—needs a lot of work. So, you finished with dinner? I can get somebody out here to clean this up and bring you a new plate. Or dessert if you want."

"Actually, I've had enough, and it's been a long day. Thank you. It was delicious."

There was an awkward pause. It was time for some humility. "So... you were right. Trying to get to Emmy on my own was useless. You already know I need your help, but I can make it official, if you want me to grovel."

"Yes. I'll help you. It's why I'm here." He lifted his hands to the sides, indicating our luxurious surroundings, as if to say *why else?*

"So then... I guess that means I'm staying here... as one of your 'fan pod members.' Where should I sleep?"

There was a new gleam in his eye that alarmed me for a moment, and I caught a hint of a suggestion from his mind—*with me*—but it was quickly whisked away, like smoke from a match that's been blown out. I wasn't even sure if it was something I'd picked up from his thoughts or if I'd imagined it.

He coughed and cleared his throat. "The other... the girls who've been recruited have their own quarters on the other side of the house, but you can keep your own room, the one where you slept last night."

I narrowed my eyes at him. "Where's *your* room?"

"Next door to that one."

"Then I'll stay in the harem."

We were both laughing as I preceded Nox into the kitchen from the deck, but the sound was drowned out by loud squealing. When Nox came in immediately behind me, the squeals turned to screams.

"Oh my God—it's him!"

"There's Nox!"

"You sure about that decision?" he muttered close behind my ear. "I don't know about you, but I'd prefer to stay as far away from *that* as possible."

"Ladies, ladies—gather round. It's not time to meet Nox yet. Please, stay together."

A tall, gorgeous woman in her early twenties with cascading dark curls spoke sternly to the new pod recruits. Then she glanced over at me. Clearly taking me for an escapee who'd gotten far too close to her master, she pointed at me and ordered, "You! Get back with the group. Stop bothering Mr. Knight."

With one last peek back over my shoulder at Nox's face, I stepped forward to join my fellow pod sisters.

Chapter Nine
Fangirl Hell

"Oh my God, he is so beautiful. Did you see those eyes?"

"I know. I've only seen him in concert, never up close except for videos. He is *way* hotter than I realized. I can't believe we're here!"

I was in fangirl Hell.

Not since my tween One Direction and Belieber phase had I experienced anything close to this. But the girls crowding my room were all my age or older, and they were acting completely over-the-top delirious about Nox.

When had he managed to glamour all of them? He'd said he hadn't even met them yet. Or maybe they were like this *without* glamour—scary thought.

"You're so lucky you got to have dinner with him. How did you pull that off?" a short baby-faced girl asked me.

"Oh... I don't know. Right place, right time, I guess."

"Well, what did he say? What's he like? Did he sing for you?" a Latina girl with glasses asked.

He *had* sung for me in the past, and if I could help it, I'd never hear him sing again—I was far too susceptible to his musical glamour. Lad had told me how different family lines of Elves had different kinds of glamour in varying strengths. Though Nox didn't seem to be able to glamour me through words alone, when he sang—well let's just say I should probably be more sympathetic about girls like these losing their minds along with all notions of free will.

"We talked—about Los Angeles, his upcoming tour, stuff like that, no big deal," I explained.

More squealing. "But he *talked* to you—like individually. How can you stay so calm? I'd die if he even looked directly at me."

There were nods and laughter all around as the others agreed. Part of me wanted to be disgusted with them, but the other part could commiserate. Maybe if I weren't a quarter Elven, I'd be just like them. That bit of Elven blood had made me immune to Nox's Sway. And Lad's. I had fallen for him the old fashioned way, much good it did me now.

When it came to Nox, I guessed I'd have to pretend to be more overwhelmed. "I'm really jet-lagged," I said, making an excuse for my previous lack of hysteria over my exclusive dinner with our pod-master. "When I get some sleep and wake up tomorrow, I probably won't even be able to believe it happened." I ended with a big smile I hoped conveyed my "excitement" at being here.

Speaking of sleep, the pod quarters were sort of like the college dorms I'd visited at Ole Miss and Mississippi State when I'd gone for tour weekends. I was in a suite with three other girls. We each had a single bed and shared a common bathroom, though this one was definitely nicer than the dorms' bathrooms had been.

My suitemates Gigi and Kim were about my age— soon-to-be high school seniors, the fourth girl, Bonnie, was in college. They were all cute and friendly, but none of them seemed to have any other ambition in life than to serve Nox and meet his fellow celebrities. Maybe they had before they'd succumbed to the glamour and forgotten everything else existed.

After we'd all introduced ourselves and chatted a bit, we took turns taking showers and getting ready for bed. It was three hours later back home in Mississippi, and I really was jet-lagged, but I didn't sleep for a long time. Instead, I lay awake thinking about Emmy.

Was she lying in bed right now in a room like this one behind those ivy-covered walls at Vallon Foster's estate? Was she homesick, or was she as happy as these girls all seemed to be? And what would happen to her between now and the time I was able to get to her, whenever that was?

This fan pod thing was worse than I'd expected. Judging from the behavior of my roomies, they would be willing to do anything and *everything* Nox wanted them to.

Like me, Emmy was a virgin—or she *had* been when she'd left home. Had she met Vallon already? Had he selected her out of his harem for his special attention one evening?

And then a new thought occurred to me—was that what *Nox* would do? Housed in separate rooms as we were, I'd have no idea if he were to summon one of his podettes to his suite. That's what they were here for, right? To serve and entertain their master?

Well, it was none of my concern if he did. As long as he helped me find Emmy, it was none of my business what he did with his time. Or these girls.

I woke to the shrieking, giggling evidence of near hysteria sounding through the hallway the next morning. Gigi opened our door to find out what was going on as Bonnie and Kim emerged from their room.

The same knockout woman from the prior night stood amid a crowd of girls in the hall, holding a clipboard.

"Ladies, Nox will be appearing on a morning TV program today. We'll need you to come along and cheer him on. Anybody ready for a bus ride to Burbank?"

You would have thought she'd announced a free trip to Maui from all the resulting commotion. Girls were jumping up and down, gripping each other's hands.

"You have one hour to dress and report for breakfast. Then we'll go to the station together. Be sure to wear your swag and bring your signs."

My suitemates ran back inside, going through their suitcases and chattering as they pulled out clothing and some other small items.

"What's that?" I asked, looking over Gigi's shoulder at the baubles in her hands.

"This is my swag. Don't you have any?"

She held the items up to me—a necklace with Nox's picture at the end, a charm bracelet with several charms. One of them was his name spelled out in black, glittery block letters, another was a guitar with "The Hidden" written on it in a cool-looking script.

Bonnie and Kim also displayed similar items—was it like the podette uniform? Later, as I stepped out into the hallway, dressed in my regular slogan-free clothes, I concluded that was exactly what it was.

The other girls were decked out in The Hidden t-shirts and swag, some carried glittery hand-made signs bearing silly sayings like "Nox Rox" and "Come Nox my sox off." I stifled giggles, embarrassed for them.

Falling into line, we filed through the mansion, first to a dining room for a quick breakfast, and then out a side door to where a private bus waited in the drive for us. The ride to the TV station seemed interminably long, partially because of the L.A. traffic, which lived up to its nasty reputation, and partially because of the unbearable fan-girling that surrounded me.

"I was one of the first applicants for his fan pod. I applied over a year ago," someone behind me said.

"Well, I applied two years ago," countered a girl from the opposite aisle.

"You did not. He wasn't even playing two years ago."

"He was! I heard some underground club recordings of the band from when he was like, sixteen."

I snorted, imagining it. The only thing that could possibly be more obnoxious than Nox at eighteen would be Nox at sixteen.

"Hey, you okay?" Gigi bumped my shoulder with hers. "You're so quiet."

"Oh. Yeah, I'm fine. I just… miss home, I guess," I said, grappling for an excuse.

Her face quirked in an expression of amusement. "Really? I haven't even thought about home." Something like melancholy ran across her face. "Until now. That's so weird. I said I'd call my mom as soon as I got here, and I haven't even called yet."

"You should." Maybe if she thought about calling home, she'd realize she didn't even have a phone anymore—maybe she'd start questioning things.

"Yeah, I really should. I'll call today, when we get back. It's all been moving so fast I guess. And everything's so exciting—don't you think?"

"It is," I said, without much enthusiasm. "What do you think we'll do at the TV station?"

She seemed to be so much more in the know than I was—they all were. Had the new pod members been given a brochure at the door or something? Maybe it was part of the glamour program.

Gigi lifted her shoulders and let them fall. "Show our love, support Nox—you know. There will be cameras everywhere. We have to show the world Nox and The Hidden are the best band ever. Maybe we'll even get on TV."

"So, we're going into the studio with him?"

"Oh, no—there's an outdoor stage. We'll be in the front few rows of the crowd."

A chill seized my heart. "He's going to *sing*?"

"Yeah, silly. He's a singer. What did you think was going to happen—juggling?"

"No. I... it's a talk show. So I thought he was going to, you know, talk to the hosts or something."

"Well, he'll probably do that, too. Oh look—there it is."

She pointed out the window to a huge modern structure topped by satellite dishes just off the highway. How many people must work in a building that big? To my eyes, the whole population of Deep River would fit into the place. The bus pulled around to the building's rear and parked.

As soon as it rolled to a stop, Amalia stood at the front and gave us our instructions. "Now this is not national TV—not yet—but it's equally as important because the eyes of the world are on California, and whatever viewers and music fans here adopt, the rest of the world wants to know about. We want everyone to know about Nox and love him as much as we do, right?"

Screams rebounded through the bus.

"No one will ever love him as much as I do!" vowed a girl one row ahead of me. I fought the urge to roll my eyes. She'd never even met him.

At Amalia's instruction, we filed down the stairs and lined up in front of a stage erected in the station's parking lot. A crowd—mostly girls but some boys, too—had already accumulated on the other side of the lot, though they were being held back from the stage area by ropes and security guards. Once we were in place, the ropes were removed, the guards stepped back, and the mob surged forward, coming to join us.

It was strange to be at a concert in the morning. Clearly everyone here had enjoyed their Toffee Mocha Frappuccinos already—the faces around me were wide awake, bright with expectation.

The warm California air was so different from the clingy humidity of Mississippi summers, but the atmosphere still felt thick with anticipation, with a buzz of excited chatter. Laughter and conversation filled my ears from every direction.

A thin bald guy dressed in all black and wearing a TV station I.D. badge and sunglasses came out onto the stage. "All right—listen up please—Darcy and Brad will be out in about five minutes. They're going to announce The Hidden, and then the band will take the stage. We want lots of enthusiasm and lots of noise—do you think we can do that?"

A chorus of screams erupted, making the guy laugh. He held both arms over his head to calm them. "Okay, okay—save some for the show." He looked down at his wristwatch and announced, "Four minutes," and then walked away toward the station's back door.

The noise died back down to an animated murmur. "Anticipation" was the wrong word for what I was feeling—the swimming sensation in my belly was more like anxiety. In a few minutes, Nox would be standing on that stage. The microphones and amps would come on, he would play his guitar. He would sing. And then I wasn't sure *what* was going to happen.

Would I lose my mind, lose my own will, behave like these girls around me? Would I become a podette for real?

I searched the area for an escape route. I was boxed in by bodies as well as our bus on one side and the back wall of the TV station on the other. Rotating all the way around to inspect the back of the parking lot, I spotted Amalia.

She was scanning the crowd with a serious expression, focused on her job. And what *was* her job exactly? Chaperone? Zoo keeper? Pimp?

Had *she* cast the glamour over my fellow pod members? She was obviously Elven, and she certainly kept a watchful eye on us all. Maybe she was combing the sea of other girls here, looking for new recruits.

Now that I thought about it, these fans were probably hoping for exactly that—to be noticed—to be chosen to become part of our elite and *privileged* group. As if to prove my point, a girl behind me tapped me on the shoulder. I turned to see her face.

"Are you in Nox's fan pod?"

I had to swallow a hard lump in my throat before answering, "Yeah."

Her curious expression melted into obvious envy. "You are *so* lucky. I didn't get in. I thought I was one of the first to sign up—they played the Roxy six months ago, and I immediately contacted his agent and left my name. I guess a lot of people did."

Reading her dejection, I almost felt sorry for her. But she had no idea how lucky she was. "I'm sorry," I said because it was the natural thing to say in a moment like that, but then I added in a lower tone, "It's not all it's cracked up to be—you should withdraw your name."

She drew back and studied my face, wide-eyed. Then her forehead creased and she nodded as if convinced. "Thanks," she said, and I watched as she moved away, pushing toward the back of the crowd, giving up her coveted spot near the stage.

Well, that was easy. I shrugged. If only it were that simple—I could just *tell* the others to pack up and go home, resume their lives and abandon the whole fan pod idea. All I could figure was that girl hadn't been glamoured yet, or not very thoroughly.

"Welcome everyone—are you ready to rock?"

The amplified voice and answering screams caused me to turn back to the stage where Barbie and Ken's real-life counterparts stood side-by-side, smiling at the crowd. The woman spoke next.

"I'm Darcy and this is Brad—we're the hosts of L.A. Morning, and it's our pleasure to welcome to the L.A. Morning stage one of the hottest new bands we've seen in a long time. They have an album dropping next month, and It. Is. Incredible."

"They really are fantastic, Darcy. I was lucky enough to see them play Whisky-a-Go-Go a few months ago, and they tore the house down." Addressing the crowd again, Brad said, "And now, without further delay...we bring you... The Hidden!"

Screams erupted around me. A drumbeat began, joined by a baseline, and the girls on each side of me began jumping like kids on Christmas morning. In fact, I doubted Santa had ever gotten such a reaction. Nox was not onstage, but his three bandmates were.

I didn't remember noticing them the night I'd seen The Hidden play in a small Oxford nightclub, but seeing them now in the bright California daylight, there was no question they were Elven.

No wonder the girls were so star-struck. The Hidden was like a boy band on steroids—each guy was perfect in his own way but more grown-up and dangerous-looking than the typical boy band member.

Naturally, they were all tall and built. The guy on keyboards was blond, a lighter shade than Lad's. He looked like he spent a lot of time on a surfboard when he wasn't performing onstage.

The drummer had longer, sandy brown hair and was shirtless, revealing a delicious tan. The base player had his dark hair cropped very short, but I knew if it had been longer, it would bear the hallmark waves of male Elven hair.

People in the crowd were screaming their names—Rolf, Anders, and Matteus from what I could understand. My eyes skipped from one to the other—it was hard to decide which one was better looking. Any of them would have easily been the cutest guy in school if he were dropped into the average American high school or college campus.

And then Nox came out on stage. And the others seemed to disappear.

The noise around me increased to a frenetic pitch that was almost deafening. The anxiety in my middle ramped up to full-on terror—this was about to happen. I had nowhere to go and no idea what my reaction to his music would be or whether I could control it. I was possibly on the verge of deep personal embarrassment.

Nox strode toward center stage with his guitar strapped around his body. He wore what must have been his usual on-stage uniform—similar to what he'd worn that night in the nightclub—a tight dark t-shirt and perfectly fitted jeans with black boots. It was weird seeing him like this. I was used to viewing him up close, through a filter of personal knowledge and distrust. But this was different.

Separated as we were by the crowd and the stage, it was almost as if I didn't know Nox, like he was someone else. Like *I* was someone else and viewing him through the eyes of the fans surrounding me. And through these new eyes… he looked amazing.

He strutted across the stage, playing the song's opening chords, his movements fluid and athletic. His face was the picture of concentration and passion as he poured himself into the music. I wanted to look away, struggled to replace the beautiful male image before my eyes with the scenes of angry confrontations that had occurred between us, but those seemed fuzzy and distant now, like dreams that slip away moments after you wake.

Nox reached the microphone stand and began to sing.

And I was lost.

As soon as the first verse came through the amps, I was under a spell. My body felt heavy and warm, anchored in place as if I might grow into the pavement beneath my feet and be content to live in his spot forever, listening to him, watching him play to the crowd.

As he sang, Nox's teeth flashed whitely, a cross between a smile and a snarl as he delivered the vocals. Now I didn't care about the reactions of the girls around me—were they still even there? I couldn't see anyone else, hear anyone else. There was only Nox and his voice washing over me in luxurious Caribbean-warm waves of sound and feeling.

He stepped back from the mic for a guitar ride and the languor lifted slightly, though the rhythmic movements of his body in time with the music captured my gaze and refused to let go.

I'd fantasized about Lad before, about what might come after the passionate kisses we'd shared. But with both of us being virgins, and never having seen a movie bearing a rating past R, I didn't have much to work with in the visuals department. Now my mind was flooded with images that made me blush, though anyone watching would assume the California heat was getting to me.

My tongue felt thick, my belly tight, my body growing warmer by the minute. I squirmed, uncomfortable in my light, non-restrictive clothing. I'd only seen Nox shirtless one time—that horrible day in Altum when I'd realized his true identity and that he'd been lying to me all along.

Now the memory came back to me in vivid detail. Worse, I saw myself in the picture, touching his bare chest, running my hands over his shoulders and down his well-muscled arms. The hot tightness in my belly increased and expanded, twisting in on itself, making me want to move, to *do something*.

Gigi, who'd apparently been standing next to me (I'd forgotten) bumped me playfully. "There you go, girl. You can *dance*."

"What?"

I looked down at my own body and realized I *was* moving to the beat of the music. Just like in the nightclub that night, I had lost control of my own body—like it wasn't *mine* anymore. Like it was *his*.

Nox resumed singing, and the full mesmerized state dropped over me again. *I hate this.* And at the same time... I loved it. The feeling of being lost in sensation, controlled by something, *someone* so much stronger than myself was strangely pleasurable. Freeing, in a way. Like I could simply let go of all my thoughts and stop worrying and drift in this enveloping bath of emotion forever.

The song ended. I felt like I might fall down, only the other fans were packed in so tightly around me I could probably have passed out and still remained on my feet. I had a quick impulse to push through the crowd, say I needed to get to the bathroom or something, and then the next song began.

This one had a slower beat, more of a ballad sound. I stared down at my feet, determined to maintain control over myself, not to look at him, not to listen—maybe I could somehow mentally block out his vocals.

But then I heard his voice—not just singing the lyrics. He *was* singing, but he was also speaking in my mind.

Ryann, are you okay?

It was him—as clear as Gigi's voice had been a few minutes ago. But when my head whipped up to look at him, Nox was singing to the crowd. His eyes narrowed in a crinkly smiling expression as he sang. Then he cut a quick side glance at me. *Dang it.* He knew I'd heard him.

And now, once again, I was really hearing him as he sang. If I'd been capable of feeling anything other than ultimate peace, I might have panicked when I recognized the song—it was the same one he'd sung the night in

Oxford when I'd tried—unsuccessfully—to leave. Just like on that night, a confusing swirl of emotions twisted through me.

Tears gathered behind my eyes. Nox's voice was the most beautiful thing I'd ever heard, his face the most beautiful thing I'd ever seen. How had I ever looked at Lad and preferred him over this masterpiece of masculine beauty? I could never leave him, never leave California, unless it was to follow him… anywhere…

A tap on my shoulder caused me to turn to the side. I blinked. Gigi's bemused expression met my eyes.

She laughed. "I've been saying your name for, like, a minute. We're supposed to go back to the bus. Come on."

I blinked again and shook my head. The concert was over? I glanced up at the empty stage, stared around me at the parking lot and the girls walking away in groups and pairs, chattering with each other about the show they'd just seen.

How long had I been… *under*? Away? Asleep? I didn't know what word to use to describe the spell that had come over me. Had there been several more songs or only those two? And where had my mind been all that time? Had I danced and screamed like an idiot? Part of me wanted to play back the recording of this show and look at the crowd shots, and part of me didn't.

This must be what full-on glamour was like. This was why a stranger could drive away with Emmy, and her mother wouldn't protest. Why people would agree to do anything they were asked.

So far no one had been able to glamour me with their words or with a look—perhaps I was resistant to that. But I was an absolute textbook case of susceptibility to musical glamour—at least to Nox's. It was terrifying to know he had so much power over me, and to admit that for now, I'd have to put up with it.

Chapter Ten
Losses

Still mortified, I followed Gigi toward the bus. As we reached the steps, someone called out, "You!"

Gigi and I both turned toward Nox's voice. He was standing beside the open door of a yellow Mercedes sports car. He pointed at me. "You, the brunette—what's your name again?"

"Uh, it's Ryann."

"Ryann. Come here—you're riding with me."

Gigi's astonished gaze flew to me, and she gave me a huge smile followed by a little shove. "Go… go!"

After a moment's hesitation, I obeyed. What choice did I have? If I told him to go to hell or even said, "No thank you," I'd be outed as a fan pod fraud.

I walked toward him, glancing back once over my shoulder at the bus. As expected, Amalia stood at the front, watching through the huge windshield.

When I met Nox at his car, I kept my voice low, though I couldn't prevent the irritation from leaking into my tone. "*What* do you want?"

"I want you to take a ride with me. Keep smiling," he instructed through his own grin. "Big Sister is watching."

Plastering on a fake smile, I tried to appear delighted as Nox walked around and opened the passenger door for me. I held onto my rant until we'd pulled out of the lot and onto the busy highway.

"What are you doing? You're not supposed to show me any special attention."

"That's not true. Alfred says the fan pod members are 'at my disposal' and I may 'use them as I wish.' I'm expected to spend time with individual girls. If I don't, it'll raise suspicion. So you're helping me keep my cover. I told my *handlers* not to expect me back for a while." He drew out the last word suggestively and raised an eyebrow at me, his mouth sliding into a sexy sideways grin.

"As long as 'keeping your cover' is all you expect me to *help* you with. Eyes back on the road," I growled, pointing through the windshield.

He laughed. "Of course. So, where do you want to go?"

As nervous as I was about being near him after the show experience, I really wasn't in a hurry to get back to fanpod headquarters and dissect The Hidden's performance with the other girls. It was exhausting to be around such hysterical enthusiasm all the time. I missed the woods, too. I wanted to go somewhere natural.

"The hills?" I suggested. "All this concrete is getting to me."

"The Hollywood hills it is. Got your hiking shoes on?"

Nox drove us up twisting streets with amazing panoramic views and parked at the Griffith Observatory.

"We can hike to the Hollywood Sign from here, if you want to," he suggested.

"Yeah. That sounds perfect, actually."

He popped the trunk and pulled out two water bottles, then led the way toward a path beyond the parking lot. The walk was only marginally challenging, steep, but with a clearly defined path and not much in the way of undergrowth—so different from hiking in the thick woods on Grandma's land. Suddenly I was suffused with the desire to be back in those woods, where I'd first met Lad, where we'd spent so many happy times together.

"So... you haven't told me what you thought of the show this morning."

I rolled my eyes over to Nox, wiping a fine sheen of sweat off my forehead. "I think you *know* the answer to that."

A sneaky grin prefaced his laugh. "Glamour-drunk is a good look for you, Ry."

I pointed at him, my finger jabbing the air in time with my emphatic words. "I will *not* be attending any more concerts, by the way."

"Ryann—"

"I mean it. That's not why I came out here, and you know it. And it's not fair for you to do that to me against my will. I *really* don't appreciate it."

Nox threw his hands out to the side, keeping pace with my new, increased walking speed. "It's not like I can help it. I didn't want any of this—the fan pods, the celebrity. I'm doing this whole thing for *you*, if you'll remember."

I glanced over at him, finding my footing easily on a flat stretch. "So, you don't want to be famous? Why sing then—why have a band and record music?"

He looked away, studying the view in the valley below through squinting eyes as he considered it. "Music doesn't feel like a choice, either. It called to me—it felt like something I *had* to do, you know? It gives me peace. It makes me happy. And when I sing... the... effects on humans... it's not something I'm trying to do. I was born with it, I guess. My parents were musical artists—our house was always filled with music. I think that's why I like California so much, why I started coming out here as soon as I was old enough to travel alone. This is where all my memories of them are. This is where we were happy as a family. I... miss that." He cleared his throat and turned his attention back to the trail ahead.

I stopped and watched his back as he went on, studied his strong calves as the incline of the path increased. I'd never spent any time considering the losses Nox had experienced.

He was an orphan. I wasn't sure how it all had come about, but I knew he'd grown up in L.A. until the age of twelve and then was forced to live in a secret underground society in the backwoods of Mississippi through no choice of his own. And from what he'd described, he'd felt like a burden or at least an interloper in Lad's home. It was a lot of upheaval for one short life, and it seemed pretty lonely.

I caught up to him. "Tell me about your parents. Can you remember them well?"

He glanced over at me warily, almost as if trying to determine whether I was sincere. Or whether I was worthy of the precious nuggets of memory I'd asked him to share. Looking back at the dusty path ahead of us, he said, "I do. I remember so much—I try to hold on to it—the past with them, being someone's son—their *real* son."

Lad had once told me his adoptive brother had always wanted what he had—that they were competitive in every arena. I had looked down on Nox when hearing those stories, but now I saw them in a different light. Nox had been just a child—he'd wanted to be loved—like any of us do.

"I'll bet your mom was pretty," I prompted. It was a safe guess—she was Elven—she had to have been pretty.

He smiled, a distant memory filling his beautiful hazel eyes. "She was. She had this long, black hair. And she had the sweetest voice. She was… Sylvie Jerrik." He glanced at me, checking to see if I recognized the name.

"Your mom was *the* Sylvie Jerrik?"

He nodded, a look of unmistakable pride on his face.

"Wow. So then your dad was…"

"Gavin Jerrik. Yeah. I told you they were musicians."

"Yeah, but I didn't realize…"

Pretty much everyone knew of the Jerriks. Gavin was one of the most prolific songwriters of the modern generation, having penned tunes for countless famous artists over the past few decades and worked as a producer with a long list of top performers. He was also known for playing several instruments in different bands through the years. And for his powerful sex appeal.

His wife was famous for her gorgeous alto voice—Mom used to say Sylvie Jerrik could sing a page out of the phone book and sell a million copies on iTunes. And that Gavin Jerrik had probably made a million conquests.

"So your last name…"

He nodded, biting his lip. "Yeah. I made up Knight."

"Stage name?"

"Something like that."

"Your dad died in a plane crash, right?"

He shrugged. "Private Lear jet. He and several other musician friends—they were on their way to perform at a festival."

"And your mom?"

"She supposedly died in the crash as well."

"But it's not true?"

He shook his head. "No, the media said so, but she and I weren't with my father on the plane. After his death, we traveled immediately to Mississippi. We left everything, in the middle of the night, the two of us. Mom took me to Altum and left me there with her sister, my aunt Mya, and then she took off again."

"Oh, I didn't realize your mom was a Light Elf."

He nodded. "Her marriage to my father was a political one to broker a peace deal—it's a common practice. But she and my father fell in love. They were happy together, and she adapted well to life among humans."

"Where is she now?"

His shoulders lifted and fell, his gaze trained on the trail ahead. "She... never came back. Which means she has to be dead, too."

"Oh my God, Nox. That's horrible. I'm so sorry." I reached out and placed a comforting hand on his arm.

He stopped walking and turned to face me. "Yeah. I guess that's the other reason I wanted to come back to California—to get some answers, try to find out what really happened."

"Have you?"

"Not yet. I haven't told anyone who my parents were—there's another reason for the fake name." He paused, a frown working its way across his forehead as if he was trying to decide how much more to say.

"What?"

"Ivar always told me I shouldn't reveal my family name. He said it might be dangerous. I chose Knight for myself when I started mixing with humans."

"I see."

"My agent Alfred asked me about my family. I almost told him, but then—I don't know—I got a strange feeling about it. I gave him a couple of made-up names. I think I have to... tread carefully or something until I know who I can trust. Like I said before—it's kind of a downer. We don't have to talk about this."

"We can if you want to," I assured him. "It's good for you to talk about them. As you said, you want to keep their memories alive. I just... I want to say you can talk to me about them anytime... if you want to."

Nox's body and expression froze, his eyes misting as they stared into mine. "Okay," he said, his voice sounding choked.

"We're here," I realized, tilting my head back to see the Hollywood sign looming above.

He looked up at the giant letters as well. They weren't quite as fancy as I'd imagined them to be—basically sheets of steel supported by steel rods sunk into concrete. I wasn't sure what I'd been expecting. Still, the idea of it was fun. No doubt Shay and my other friends back home would think it was cool I'd seen the sign up close.

When we'd hiked back to the car, Nox opened my door for me partway but stopped mid-motion.

"I'm sorry," he said. "For keeping the truth from you. I did feel bad about it, but... well, I'm really glad you know now. I mean, I guess I am a Dark Elf by birth, but I don't really feel like these are my people. Not yet anyway. And like I told you, I've never felt truly a part of the Light Elves either. I've been kind of a loner. It's nice to have a friend."

Swallowing back a lump in my throat, I said, "I understand. Thanks for apologizing." I broke eye contact and looked at the ground until the car door was completely open, then got in and let out the breath I'd been holding.

So there it was. We were friends now. In spite of what he'd done in the past, he was helping me. I understood him a little better. And all we had out here was each other.

When Nox was behind the wheel, I turned to him. "You realize we're going to have to keep our friendship under wraps while we're here. We can't keep running off together. You're going to have to spread your *attention* around."

He nodded and started the engine with a smirk and a lifted brow. "How do you know I haven't been?" Then the smug look dissolved into a true smile. "Just kidding. I guess you're right, though."

I laughed. "Most guys would be more excited. You've got a houseful of adoring women at your beck and call. They're all really cute."

"And they're all really squealy. I didn't even know voices could *go* that high." He laughed, but his expression turned serious as he drove the car down the winding road toward the valley. "It's weird to be worshipped. It makes me uncomfortable."

"Yeah—I guess you're not *quite* a Dark Elf yet, then. You'd better get used to it. It's only going to get worse because it doesn't look like you're going to get *less* famous."

Nox joined the pod in the enormous dining room for dinner that night, sitting at a table at the front of the room with Amalia. I tried not to glance in their direction too often, but most of the girls around me stared throughout pretty much the entire meal.

"Do you think they're a thing?" Kim asked in a low voice, studying Nox and Amalia speaking together.

"Celeb Tonight said he's single," Bonnie argued. "Besides, if they were a thing, she'd probably be pissed he went hiking with Ryann today."

"Well, Amalia wasn't exactly *happy* when she saw them leave together," Gigi said.

I whipped my glance to her. "Really? Did she say something?" I knew Amalia wasn't jealous, but I *was* worried about her watching anything I did too closely.

"She didn't *say* anything—she just shot you the death glare as you two drove off. I'd watch my back around her."

Bonnie nodded. "Yeah, she is pretty scary. She told us to think of her like a big sister, but she seems more like a warden or something."

"Are you thinking about going home?" I asked.

Bonnie looked at me like I'd suggested she try to suck her grilled chicken entrée through a straw. "God no. I'm living in Nox Knight's *house*. This is my chance to get to know him and go to amazing parties and have the life I've always wanted. Nothing and no one could make me leave."

"Me too," Gigi agreed.

"Me three," Kim added.

I was about to say something to inject some doubt, but at that moment, Nox stood and lifted his hands. "Ladies. Ladies, if I could get your attention for a minute."

A hush fell over the dining room.

"I want to thank you all for being here and for your support this morning at the show. You made it really fun for me and the band. And even though we're only getting started, I have to say… I think I have the best fan pod out there."

The room erupted in applause and screams of delight. Nox smiled and left his table, crossing the room to a table of six girls toward the front. I couldn't hear what was being said, but it looked like he asked their names because each one of them spoke in turn, red-faced and beaming. After about a minute, he lifted a hand to a pretty blonde in an apparent invitation.

Her spread palm went to her chest. It wasn't hard to read her shocked expression or her lips. "Me?" she gasped.

He smiled and waited until she rose from her seat and made her way around the table to take his hand. An odd hot sensation twisted through my belly when his fingers wrapped around hers. I averted my gaze from the two of them as they left the dining room together.

Where were they going? What would they talk about? What would they do together and for how long? And why in the world did I care?

I finally lifted my eyes from my untouched plate. My tablemates were staring at me.

"Are you okay?" Gigi asked in a hushed tone.

What should I say? Glancing around at their expectant expressions, I considered it. How would a *real* fan podette, under the influence of powerful Elven glamour, react? Should I be blasé... or pretend to be jealous?

Maybe I didn't have to pretend. The strange sensation had spread from my belly to my chest where it burned hotly, serving as rocket fuel for my accelerated heartbeat.

I lifted my shoulders and let them fall, keeping my eyes trained on the plate of unfinished food in front of me. "Whatever," I bit out, allowing the venom I tasted to leak into the word. "It's not like we're *together* or anything."

Gigi reached over and patted my back. "At least you'll get to see him at the Hidden's show tomorrow night."

I shrugged away from her consoling touch. "I'm not going."

"What?" Bonnie said. "But... you have to. We all have to. That's what we're here for." The look in her round blue eyes reminded me of the dazed, vacant expression on the face of Emmy's mother on the day she disappeared. *Glamoured.* Right. I'd have to watch myself or my new friends would start wondering why I was so different. Worse, I'd draw the attention of those who *weren't* my friends.

I glanced toward the head table where Amalia now sat alone. She scanned the room, and to my relief, her eyes passed right over me. I was invisible on her radar. For my own good, and for Emmy's, I needed to keep it that way.

CHAPTER ELEVEN
SWAY

Amalia sent us out to the beach the next morning. I guessed it was good for Nox's image to have a bevvy of bathing beauties decorating the shoreline outside his home. If they sported freshly sun-kissed skin—even better.

Like the other girls, I wore a bikini, though mine was comprised of considerably more fabric than most. Fortunately, I'd packed a good supply of sunblock. While the air felt cooler, the California sun seemed stronger than Mississippi's summer rays. Maybe because here the UVA and UVB weren't fighting through so many layers of humidity to get to my skin.

The day was bright and crisp. I'd never seen a sky so blue and cloudless. Settling onto a beach towel, I attempted to read a paperback but couldn't keep my focus on the story. A nearby conversation kept hijacking my attention. The curvy blonde who'd been *chosen* by Nox last night was recounting her evening to her suitemates.

"He was *so* sweet. And his room is *amazing*. Oh my God, you should see the size of his *bed.*"

Suddenly sweltering under the midday rays, I leapt to my feet. No doubt spraying sand from my digging strides, I went to the water's edge and charged into the surf, diving under the sparkling blue surface. *Oh dang this is cold.*

I'd never swum in the Pacific before, having grown up much closer to the sugar sand and turquoise waters of Florida beaches. While the Gulf of Mexico was like a warm bath, this was more like a cold shower. Which was perfect. I *needed* a good shock to the system to clear out all the crazy images going through my head.

After a few minutes of wading deeper and deeper, my body acclimated to the bracing water temperature. I began swimming laps perpendicular to the shoreline, glancing back every once in a while at the huge beach home to get my bearings. The blonde's story seemed to have drawn a crowd. A group of girls sat in the sand around her, no doubt fascinated by the details of her night with the Rock God.

I plunged my face back into the water for one, two strokes, determined not to let myself speculate on those details, on what might have occurred in Nox's room, in his reportedly enormous bed.

What is the matter with me? I could care less what Nox did with the other girls, beyond concern for their well-being as brainwashed glamour victims, of course.

"Having a nice swim?"

I stopped mid-stroke and choked on a mouthful of salt water I'd suddenly inhaled at the sound of the silky male voice beside me.

Nox laughed and pounded my back with a warm fist as he treaded water and supported me with his other hand. "Sorry, didn't mean to startle you. Guess you were pretty focused on your laps there."

I coughed again, finally expelling enough seawater to respond. My voice was scratchy and annoyed-sounding. "Where did you come from?"

"I got in down the beach there." Pointing toward a rocky outcropping in the distance, he smiled and rolled his eyes toward the horde on the beach in front of his house. "Wanted to get in a swim before facing the feeding frenzy."

I nodded. "Probably wise you didn't walk out your back door in a Speedo. You might never have made it to the water."

He laughed out loud. "If you ever catch me in a Speedo, you have my *permission* to feed me to the sharks. So, how are you this morning? Sleep well last night?"

"Fine," I lied, unwilling to admit to the dreams that had plagued me throughout the night. Dreams where Nox's dark head bent over a small platinum one and the scene progressed from there.

"Well, that's good, because the show's gonna go pretty late tonight. It's at the Viper Room, and things don't even get *started* there until around ten."

I treaded water in front of him, both of us bobbing with the swell and ebb of the ocean. When the current pushed me toward Nox, I fanned the water with my arms to force my body back and prevent our limbs from tangling. "I told you already—I'm not going to any more of your shows."

"Ryann." He sighed in exasperation. "What if I promise not to use my glamour?"

I narrowed my eyes. "I don't think so. You've already admitted you're not in control of it. You said it happens naturally."

"Well… I might have *some* control…" he said with a sheepish grin. "You know what I mean. You must feel yourself exerting your Sway. Can't you dial it up or down when you want to?"

"My *sway*? What are you talking about?"

"Well… you're part Elven. You must have *some* glamour. And I've seen how the other girls in the house react when you make a suggestion. I think your glamour must be persuasion—we call it the Sway. All of us have it to some degree, but certain Elves have a special gift for using it."

I shook my head, squinting against the glare of the sun's reflection off the water around us. "No. I don't feel anything. And if I did have any glamour, wouldn't it be the same as my grandma's? Lad said it comes through family lines. If I had to guess, I'd say Grandma Neena's glamour is empathy. Mom seems to have it, too, although she doesn't even know she's half Elven."

"Are you especially aware of others' emotions then?" Nox asked.

"I never thought so—not any more than most people are. But then I guess we don't really know how other people experience things. Maybe they're *not* sensing as much as I am about people's feelings. I don't know."

"Well, you should try to figure it out—ask your grandmother—being in touch with your glamour abilities might come in handy out here." He gave me a wicked smile. "Want to try out your empathy on me? What am I feeling right now?"

His expression told me whatever he was feeling—I was better off not knowing. I splashed water at his face, making him blink in surprise and then laugh out loud. "So you *can* read my feelings, huh?"

"We'll *both* be feeling hypothermia if we don't get out of this icy water soon," I growled.

"*This is nice.* You should feel it at night—I wouldn't swim out here after dark if you paid me."

"Well, I'm freezing. See you back on shore." I knifed one hand then another through the ocean, aiming for the beach and *away* from Nox and his too-loud feelings.

A swirl of water rushed over my legs as his powerful kick propelled him past me. "How about a race to warm your blood?" He called back over his shoulder.

Kicking harder, I gained on him but there was no out-swimming him. Nox emerged from the ocean a few yards ahead of me and right onto the most populated part of the beach. He was not wearing a Speedo, but a pair of orange board shorts, slung low on his hips and revealing an expanse of tanned skin across his wide shoulders and well-formed back.

Damn these Elven guys. Did they really have to have glamour *and* be gorgeous? The human race didn't stand a chance.

I couldn't see the front view, but the girls on the beach could, and it was obvious from their expressions the scenery was impressive. Literally every one of them stared at Nox as if they were starving and he was made of chocolate. And yes, at that moment, I was pretty sure I *could* read emotions—pure 100-proof desire swelled from each pair of feminine eyes.

Glancing back over his shoulder at me first, Nox plopped down in the sand next to a cute Latina girl and her blanket mate. They giggled and said "hello," but that's all I heard of the conversation because I kept on walking, going to the stairs and up to the back patio of Nox's house.

I'd had enough of him and his particular brand of *Sway* for one day. And if he thought I was going to the Viper Room to hear him play tonight, he had another thing coming.

Pushing open the French doors to the house, I stepped inside, wiping my feet on the mat to remove any traces of sand and water. I hadn't stopped to grab my towel and didn't want to leave drips along the path from the back door to my room.

"What are you doing?" The chilly female voice emanated from the kitchen.

I whirled to face Amalia's sternly beautiful face. "Uh, coming in?"

"This is beach time." Her tone told me "beach time" had been an order not a suggestion. An order I'd unwittingly disobeyed.

"I know. I needed to uh... use the bathroom."

"There's one in the pool house you could have used." She studied me through a narrow gaze. "Where are you *from*, Ryann?"

I began to sweat, though the house was pleasantly cool inside. Was Amalia's glamour lie-detection? If it was, if there even was such a thing, I couldn't lie to her. But if I told her the truth, would she read anything into the fact that I'd come here from the same town where Nox had been living for the past five years?

I opted for honesty. "Mississippi." And added a little something extra. "I hope I never have to go home—I love Los Angeles."

"And Nox, too, I assume?" Her eyebrow lifted in a challenge.

"Oh yes," I gushed in my best approximation of my fan pod sisters. "He's so perfect. I almost died when I saw him out there on the beach. He's in a swimsuit, and his body is so—"

"Go straight to the bathroom," she snapped, cutting me off. "Don't dally or wander around the house. And then get back outside with the others—and *stay* with the others unless Nox or I direct you otherwise." I turned to go but her voice stopped me. "And Ryann? I have my *eye* on you."

A chill chased down my back as I nodded and padded to the hallway bathroom in my bare feet. Something about the way she'd said it made me believe there was more to her last comment than making sure I didn't wander through the house or get separated from my podmates.

She was suspicious of me. Could she tell I wasn't glamoured, that I was here not to worship Nox, but with my own agenda?

Standing at the sink a few minutes later, I washed my hands and studied my sunburned face in the mirror. "Dang it," I whispered as it hit me. Thanks to my untimely bathroom visit, Amalia had noticed me. She knew my name. She would in all likelihood notice if I wasn't there tonight.

Ugh. There was no way out of it. I'd have to go to Nox's show.

CHAPTER TWELVE
VIPERS

I'd heard of the Viper Room before, but nothing I'd imagined could have prepared me for the real thing. The iconic music club on the Sunset Strip was as dark and moody on the inside as its black-painted exterior suggested.

We were brought in through the back door, which I gathered was some sort of privilege, because the huge doorman told two groups ahead of us, "You gotta enter from the front."

Inside, I took in the big, u-shaped red leather booths, the long bar, the black acoustic tile ceiling, the heat of the large crowd already gathered there. The place smelled like the inside of a shot glass, and the noise level was so different from the outside I had to fight the urge to cover my ears with my hands.

It was only my second time inside a bar, and this was a far cry from the small club just off Oxford, Mississippi's town square. The crowd here had a seasoned feel to it, like these people had heard more music and seen more celebrities than any of us ever would. They were casually dressed but all had a city-cool feel to them. Tattoos and piercings were plentiful. Many of the girls sported a wild, sexy, rock-chick vibe, wearing lots of black with either stilettos, or on the other end of the scale, Chuck Taylors.

A wide dance floor skirted the raised semi-circle stage, which was occupied at the moment by a pop punk band. The four members all wore t-shirts and jeans and looked like the boys in your high school who seemed nice but whose names you could never quite remember—skinny, clean cut, young for their age. They were in their element tonight, bouncing around the stage with their instruments, sweating, and filling the club with sound and energy. They were good, but they were clearly human. If the crowd liked *them*, how would they react to Nox and his Elven bandmates?

Though I hadn't seen him yet, I assumed Nox was somewhere in the building because he'd left the house before our bus did to join his band for setup. Amalia had told us on the way over The Hidden wasn't the main act tonight—they'd play somewhere in between these guys and a much-more-famous alternative rock band.

The booths were completely full as were the black bench seats around the perimeter of the bar area. That left the dance floor, so that's where my pod sisters and I were herded. Some of the girls must have gotten the dress code memo because they blended right in with the L.A. hipster crowd. Others of us looked like the out-of-place small town girls we were, in our sundresses and sandals. We all moved to the music as we watched the band, watched the people around us.

I didn't have a fake I.D., but Gigi must have because she pressed an icy beer bottle against my bare arm then laughed and handed it to me when I yelped.

"Thanks. How did you even make it to the bar? It's packed in here," I yelled to be heard over the music.

"I'm from Las Vegas," she said by way of explanation as if being born in that city imbued a person with some sort of special bar-navigation skills.

I nodded, pretending to understand. "So, what do you think of these guys?"

"They're okay," she shouted back. "But I'm only here to see *one* man. I hope he's up next." Her raised brows and naughty smile told me she was referring to our host.

As if on cue, the punk boys finished their last song with a crash of guitars and drums, screamed their thanks into the mics and encouraged everyone to tip their bartenders and give a warm welcome to The Hidden.

The welcome was more than warm. It couldn't have been the first time the band had played this venue. There was too much anticipation. The screams from the crowd were actually louder than those of the fan pod, which was saying something because my eardrums were nearly blown out simultaneously by the two girls on either side of me.

As before at the TV show performance, the shirtless drummer—Rolf was his name—and two other band members, Anders and Matteus, took the stage first. Rolf started a driving beat, and Matteus joined in with a steady, sexy baseline, his face deadly serious. Anders, on the other hand, flashed the crowd a blinding grin as he played a keyboard run, setting up the melody for the first song.

Beside me, Gigi started screaming. She wasn't *totally* oblivious to the charms of the other guys. I giggled at her reaction.

And then Nox stepped into the light, grabbing the microphone and immediately launching into a long, achy note that shot through my brain, ricocheted off my heart, and settled into the pit of my stomach where it set off a chain reaction of shivers and heat.

He grabbed his guitar and began administering chords and notes without one shred of restraint or mercy. Cradling the body of the instrument with one hip, he leaned back then forward as he played, working the stage, wearing an expression that made me blush with its journey from pain to ecstasy. He was lost in the music already, and I. Was. Screwed.

I should have known he wouldn't be able to resist using his glamour on a night like this, in a place like this, in front of a crowd like this. Maybe he'd never intended to resist, had only said that this morning to get me here.

Well, here I was, and for at least the next forty-five minutes, I'd be under Nox's spell. Maybe it wouldn't be so bad this time. I'd been through it before and survived. Maybe I'd built up some sort of immunity or something.

Nox reached for the microphone again, and *oh God* I was *not* immune.

If anything, the effect of his singing on me was worse than ever. Instead of dialing down his power, he'd apparently cranked it to full capacity. Maybe he wasn't as in control of it as he believed—he seemed immersed in the song itself, oblivious to his effect on the club-goers.

All around me girls reacted in ways that would cause them deep mortification if only they were aware, and I was powerless to defend myself from committing similarly embarrassing acts. As the band's set went on, it only got worse. I did *not* want to blank out the way I had the other day in the TV station parking lot. But it was probably going to happen—I couldn't even begin to remove myself from this situation.

I wanted to go outside for some air. I wanted to go back to Mississippi. I wanted to rip Nox's clothes off and taste every inch of his glistening skin.

No, no, no. I have to fight it.

Song after song, I battled ferociously for self-control and dignity preservation. My new prayer became *not* that the performance would end, but that *when* it did, I wouldn't have any opportunity to be near Nox.

Because if I *was* around him—if he sought me out after the show for any reason—I'd be in big trouble. I would do anything he wanted me to. I might even be the aggressor, losing control of myself and mauling him like one of these crazed fangirls.

The cool glass surface of another beer bottle pressed against my wrist, and I looked to the side to see a cute twenty-something guy standing beside me. He had a preppy, college-boy look about him with light eyes and messy brown hair. He smiled, and the fog lifted from my brain slightly.

"Want this? You look hot." He winked to cue me to his double entendre.

"Oh, thanks, but I've got one..." Glancing down at the empty bottle in my other hand I realized I'd finished it. And I was super thirsty. "Actually, I'll take it—thanks." I smiled at the guy and lifted the bottle to my lips. No one had ever bought me a drink before.

He drank from his own bottle then leaned closer to me, struggling to communicate over the volume of the music. "What's your name? I'm Mickey."

"Hi. I'm Ryann."

"Hi." He grinned again. "Where you from?"

I tried twice to tell him, but he didn't seem to be able to understand me with all the club noise. He shook his head and tapped his ear.

"Want to go out and get some fresh air for a minute?" he asked.

I glanced at the exit door then back at the stage where Nox was completing a guitar solo and edging toward the mic again. A break from the music and his glamour was exactly what I needed—for a minute or *longer*.

"Yeah." I nodded to Mickey, and he grabbed my hand, turning so our fingers were joined behind his back as he led me through the crowd toward the front entrance.

Stepping out onto the sidewalk was like breaking through a barrier between worlds. The heavy door closed behind us, and the brightness and noises of the busy street replaced the dark musical allure of The Hidden and its front man entirely.

I took in a deep draught of night air, relieved to be free of the intoxicating music. But I still didn't feel quite myself.

Though I'd had only the one light beer and a sip of the one Mickey had given me, I felt drunk—no, not drunk exactly—but definitely not sober. I stumbled a bit on the sidewalk and Mickey's arms came around me, steadying me.

"You all right, baby?"

"Yeah." I nodded, embarrassed, and tried to pull away from him toward the club's exterior wall, intending to lean against it for support.

Mickey didn't loosen his hold, but took a few steps with me until we both reached the building. Looking up from the sidewalk, I saw we weren't actually in front of the club anymore but against a side wall in a small alley of sorts. I was grateful for the relative darkness because the streetlights and headlights had begun to blur and grow spokes as if they were starbursts instead of circles of light.

I blinked slowly, trying to clear my eyes. "I'm sorry," I said. "I don't usually drink, so—"

"No worries. So where were you saying you come from?"

"Mississippi." I had to fight to form the syllables of my home state's name correctly with my tired tongue. "A small town there."

"Ah." He grinned widely. "A farm girl—I thought so. I'll bet you came out here to break into modeling, right?"

I shook my head, wanting to argue. A small town and a farm weren't the same thing. And being tall and being a model *really* weren't the same things. But before I could put the words together, Mickey was asking me another question, leaning close to my ear, though it was unnecessary since I could hear perfectly well out here in the relative quiet.

"You come here with a couple friends?" His nose nudged my cheek as he spoke, and the fumes of something much stronger than beer wafted across my nostrils.

I pulled my head back to re-establish some distance between us. My hair brushed the rough wall behind me. "Yes. More than a couple, actually, a whole bunch. I'm in Nox Knight's fan pod—we came together."

"Right. I saw that whole mob of hotties come in at once. Must be hard for them to keep track of all of you in a place like this."

I nodded in agreement, a small part of my foggy brain wondering at the strangeness of his observation. That same part of me propelled me away from the wall and toward the opening of the alley, toward the shiny busyness of the West Hollywood thoroughfare.

"I should go back inside. They're probably looking for me. And I need to sit down."

At that moment, my knees buckled. I would've dropped to the pavement if Mickey hadn't caught me and propped me back against the wall, pinning me upright with the front of his body.

"Whoops, Farm Girl. Almost lost you there. You *are* a lightweight, aren't you?" He laughed. "I shouldn't have wasted a whole one on you."

My head swam with confusion. *I'm not a farm girl.* And wait—*a whole one*—*whole what?* I tried to ask him what he meant, but my mouth was refusing to work for some reason. And my eyelids felt like heavy garage doors. It took all my strength to pry them open again.

What I saw was an evil-looking grin on Mickey's formerly friendly face. And then the nasty smile was moving closer. His mouth landed on my neck, fastening on the tender skin with too much force and making me squirm from its gross wetness.

Oh God. I was going to have a huge hickey from a make-out session with a guy I didn't even know or like. This wasn't what I'd planned for the evening. How had I gotten myself into this situation? Having my brains glamoured out by Nox was looking harmless by comparison.

I pushed weakly against Mickey's chest with my dead-feeling arms. He pulled his mouth away enough to mutter, "You want to touch me, baby? Go right ahead. Here, I'll help you out."

Gripping my wrists, he pulled both my hands down the front of his body and held them against his crotch before diving at the other side of my neck and working his way to my collarbone with lewd, open-mouthed kisses.

"No," I managed to say, struggling to get away from him. He was shorter than me but far stronger. The more I struggled, the harder he pressed me against the wall. My lungs fought to pull in the necessary air for consciousness.

He began to move his lower body against me, groaning with enjoyment. That's when the real fear set in. A surge of adrenaline pushed through the stupor and enabled me to cry out.

"Stop! Get off me."

I pulled my hands from his grasp and got in one weak slap. His body jerked back abruptly—far too forcefully to be the result of my powerless strike. Someone else was in the alley with us. A sickening crack sounded as a blow landed against Mickey's face.

He stumbled backward, one hand to his jaw. "What the hell?"

Shocked, I whirled to see his assailant, stumbled myself, and nearly fell down. It was Nox.

But… he's on stage. How could he be…

"What are you doing to her?" Nox demanded.

Mickey righted himself and pasted on a placating smile. He took a step toward Nox with both hands raised in the surrender position. "Hey, we were just having a good time, man. No big deal."

Nox bit out the next words through clenched teeth. "She can barely stand."

"Well, my girl's a little drunk, but—" Mickey's explanation was cut off by another blow, this one to the nose, and his body fell back, hitting the other wall of the alley.

"She's not *your* girl," Nox said with quiet determination. He spun away from his dazed opponent and came to me then, gripping my upper arm and staring into my face with a fierce expression.

"Ryann—are you okay? What did he do to you?" He glanced over my body then his hand came to my face as he searched my eyes.

I shook my head, trying to reassure him, but I probably only sounded as confused as I was. "I… I'm fine. I think. I guess I'm drunk."

"Why did you come out here alone with him? Don't you realize how dangerous that was?" His tone was ragged with anger and some other emotion. It was hard to analyze anything in my muddled state.

"I don't know. I guess I… needed a break?"

He stilled. "From me? Oh man. You needed a break from me." His eyelids closed and his head dropped back on his shoulders. Opening his eyes and fixing them on mine, he said, "I'm so sorry. I know I told you I wouldn't—damn it—this is bad. You almost got hurt because of me. If I hadn't seen you leave with him—" He broke off the sentence and swore again, this time more colorfully.

"Wait… why are you out here? What's going on in there? With the show?" I asked.

He waved a hand at the club wall as if the show no longer mattered. "Drum solo. Rolf is having the time of his life. You okay to walk?" He pulled me against his side and began leading me toward the front of the club. "We'd better get back in there, before—"

"What's going on out here?" a harsh female voice demanded.

Lifting my heavy head from Nox's shoulder, my eyes met the glare of Amalia. She was flanked by several podettes, all of them wide-eyed at the unconscious man behind me and the sight of Nox's bloody knuckles.

"I can't believe you left during a set," she scolded him. "And got in a fight? What were you thinking?"

His face molded into a sarcastic mask. "Well, let me see, Amalia—I guess I was thinking one of my girls was about to get raped in an alleyway and that perhaps that wouldn't be a *positive* thing."

"What's so special about this one?" She looked down her nose at me, her eyes sparking with suspicion.

Nox raised his voice. "Nothing. It's just I don't like some asshole thinking he can take what's mine. And they're *all* mine." He reached out and drew a girl with a high ponytail to his side, draping a long arm over her shoulders. "What's the point of having my own fan pod if I have to share my girls with some roofie-pushing frat boy?"

Looking somewhat mollified, Amalia relaxed her posture. "Well, I know you're new to this, but it's not your job to keep up with them. Leave that to me—you take care of the music—let me take care of your girls."

"Well then *take care of them*," he growled. He shoved me into her arms and strolled toward the club's entrance, dropping his hand to ponytail-girl's behind for a frisky squeeze. She laughed and looked up at him in delighted surprise.

I dropped my gaze and allowed Amalia to lead me back into the club. She somehow found a vacant spot on a bench and steered me into it. Chucking me under the chin to raise my face, she stared directly into my eyes and said, "You will stay here and not move until I tell you to."

"Yes," I said, hoping that was the appropriate response to her obvious attempt to glamour me.

A few minutes later, Gigi appeared with a bottle of water. "Here. Amalia said you're supposed to drink this. Are you okay? What happened out there?"

"Nothing. Nothing happened." *But something could have.* I shuddered, suddenly cold inside the hot nightclub.

It occurred to me the Dark Elves and their schemes were not the only evil to be found here in the big city. I'd been so eager to get away from Nox's glamour I'd placed myself smack in the path of a dangerous human.

Who would've thought I'd be better off *with* Nox than without him?

Chapter Thirteen
News From Home

"Where am I? What's happening?" I bolted forward in my seat and looked around me wildly, clutching my belly at a sudden wave of nausea.

"You're okay. You're on the bus. You dozed off."

Gigi's voice from beside me pulled me back to reality. I collapsed back into my seat, trying to relax. My heart was on a spinning hamster wheel, and I was covered in a fine sheen of sweat. High blood pressure made my eyes feel like they were about to pop.

"How long was I out?"

"About half an hour. We're almost home. What did you smoke with that guy?" Gigi didn't sound disapproving, only curious.

"What?" I jerked my head around to face her, triggering a fresh sickening wave. "I didn't smoke *anything*."

"Oh." She nodded with a perceptive look. "He buy you a drink?"

"A beer."

"Yep. He probably slipped some keta in there—or a roofie—but I think if it was that, you wouldn't have woken up for a while yet."

"What's keta?"

"Ketamine. Another date rape drug. It's used in emergency rooms, but I know some kids who use it as a club drug. It comes in a powder for smoking. But it also comes in a liquid. I'll bet he put a dose in your beer. It works fast, but it wears off pretty fast, too. By the way, you shouldn't drink anything in a club you didn't buy and open yourself... or get from *me*." She grinned.

"*Now* you tell me." I sighed. I closed my eyes again and tried to do some heart-slowing, stomach-calming deep breathing, attempting to picture the serene woods surrounding Grandma Neena's log house. I missed home desperately. In my mind, I walked the paths of her land, sunlight peeping through the leafy canopy above me, the trickling music of a natural spring emptying into a crystal clear pool nearby.

It was working until the watery melody somehow segued into a guitar riff, and my peaceful mental getaway brought me full circle back to the Viper Room where the last scene I'd witnessed was Nox and the guys standing in front of the adoring crowd, accepting their applause at the end of their final set.

One of the pod girls, overcome with excitement, had jumped up onto the stage and hugged Nox. With a wolfish grin, he'd asked her, "What's your name sweetheart?"

"Robin," she'd breathed into the mic.

"Come here, Robin." And he'd pulled the girl against him and kissed her mouth hard and long and with a level of enthusiasm that could have left no doubt in Amalia's mind—or anyone else's for that matter—he was more than happy to spread himself around when it came to his fan pod. We were *all* special to him... for a few minutes.

Whatever. So far this whole thing had been a big fat bust. What did I even think I was doing here? I'd nearly gotten myself assaulted tonight. I was no closer to finding Emmy. I was completely out of my element and inadequate for the task. If I *did* have any glamour, I wasn't sure how to use it or whether *empathy* could even be useful.

I would have to ask Grandma about her gifts, and I felt a sudden, desperate desire to talk to my mom. I missed them both terribly. Daddy, too.

I needed to hear a friendly voice, to talk to someone I could actually trust. For the thousandth time, I wished Lad had found it in his heart to come to L.A. with me and help me find Emmy. But then, I guessed he wasn't someone I could count on anymore, either.

After my roommates fell asleep around three o'clock, I waited a few extra minutes then crept to our door and out into the hall. I felt like a ghost, slipping through the dark hallways in my short white nightgown, the only sleepwear I'd brought on this trip.

Once I made it to the back door and out onto the deck, I sat on the warm wood with my back against the house and gazed out at the rolling waves. They looked almost black in the moonlight.

Glancing up at the darkened windows along the back of the house, I hoped Amalia was sleeping, too. Where were her quarters? Hopefully nowhere nearby. Nox had told me the mansion had two master suites, so I assumed she'd taken one of them. The other was his of course.

Because I'd arrived here separately from the other pod girls *sans*-glamour, I'd been able to bring my own phone, which I'd been keeping powered off and hidden in a pocket of my overnight bag to avoid detection. Now I turned it on and dialed our home number. It was three hours later in Mississippi—early morning her time—and Grandma Neena was an early riser. At least I hoped she was awake. I really needed to talk to someone.

"Ryann? Ryann honey, I'm so glad to hear from you," she said as soon as she'd picked up the phone.

I smiled, feeling tears spring up in my eyes. "Hi Grandma. It's good to hear your voice, too. How are you?"

"Well, I'm just fine, honey. My garden's looking good, and things are starting to really come together at the factory for Magnolia Sugar Tea."

"That's good," I said without much enthusiasm.

"You sound upset. What's wrong?"

"Nothing. Well, honestly, a lot of things. I haven't found Emmy yet, and I'm homesick. And…" *I almost got date raped tonight.* "I feel… really alone." My voice cracked on the last word, making me sound like a bereft nine year old.

"Aw, darlin'. I'm sorry. Isn't Nox helping you?"

"Not yet. I'm not sure if he knows how to. And they're keeping him really busy with all the music stuff. I don't know… maybe this wasn't a good idea."

"Don't give up yet honey. Give Nox a chance. He said it might take time, didn't he?"

He had, but I wasn't sure how much I could believe of what Nox said. He'd also said he wasn't into the fan pod thing and was only doing it to help me, but he'd certainly seemed into it tonight up on the stage with Robin.

"Is Mom up yet?"

"Actually… she's not here. She spent the night with Davis."

Something in her tone made me probe further. "Is something going on?"

"Well, I'll let her tell you. But maybe you should call your daddy today. I bet he'd love to hear from his girl."

Uh oh. Something was definitely going on. "Grandma… tell me."

"Well… she and Davis are pretty serious, and I guess they're ready to… make things official."

"Oh my God. Is she engaged?"

"Like I said, darlin', talk to her—it's her news to share."

"All right. I'm gonna get off the phone and call Daddy before he goes to work. I don't get that much phone time here. Oh wait—I wanted to ask you about your glamour. What kind do you have? What's your... specialty or whatever?"

"Oh. I didn't expect that one. It's emotional acuity, some call it empathy. Why?"

"Yeah. I figured. Do you think I have any?"

"I certainly do. You've been highly attuned to other people's feelings since you were a bitty thing—your parents were always commenting on it. Of course neither one of them knew it was glamour."

"Do you have... any other ones?"

"Well, no. We only have one each, generally."

"But it's *possible* to have more than one?"

"Why are you asking about this now?"

"Well, Nox seems to think my glamour is Sway—persuasion, you know? But how's that possible if our family line has empathy?"

Silence on the other end of the connection made me wonder if our call had been lost. "Grandma? You still there?"

"Yes. Yes, I was just thinking—I have seen a few instances where someone might end up with more than one glamour strength. I guess we'll have to wait and see what develops for you. Don't worry about it. It'll be clear to you when the time is right."

"Okay, well I'm going to call Daddy—"

"Ryann?"

"Yes?"

"There's one more thing—I'm not sure if I should say anything…"

"Well, you've already started—so tell me."

There was a long pause—I guess she was still uncertain. "I talked to Lad, honey."

A sinking feeling pulled at me, making my head heavy and my lungs labor for enough breath to respond. "When… what did he say?"

"I went to Altum to visit my family last night. I saw him there… with Vancia… the girl he—"

"I know who she is."

"Well, I guess the wedding is back on."

Now the whirling, sinking feeling was a full-blown cyclone. I'd known Lad was out of my life. But this—this was it—forever—for good. Clenching my jaw and squeezing my eyelids together, I tried not to picture Lad's beautiful bride, but there she was, in all her platinum-haired, luminous Elven glory.

After a long silence on the line, Grandma finally spoke again. "I'm sorry, honey. I thought you might need to hear that. Should I not have told you?"

"No. You were right—I… I think I did need to hear it. I'm glad you told me."

"You're going to be okay, Ryann. Things will work out as they're supposed to."

"Okay," I whispered. "I miss you. Love you."

"Love you, too, darlin'."

I sat with the phone in my lap for a few minutes, listening to the surf stirring the sand beyond the deck, and considered not calling my dad after all. I didn't really want to talk anymore. In fact, I didn't feel like doing anything at all. Maybe I could stay here forever and grow into the deck like a barnacle. Finally, I did dial his number—Grandma *had* hinted he wasn't doing well and that I should check on him.

Rather than lifting my spirits, the phone call with Daddy left me even more depressed. He didn't tell me outright that Mom and Davis were engaged, but he was so morose I couldn't draw any other conclusion.

"I shouldn't have left," he kept saying. "I should have stayed and worked things through. That way she never would have even run into him. She would never have seen him again."

He was rambling, and he sounded like he might have been hung over—maybe even still drinking at six a.m. I felt horrible for him. I could relate to the near delirium being finally-and-forever dumped could bring on. I'd barely been able to breathe, much less think straight after Lad had broken things off with me for good.

And it didn't matter *if* it was somehow "for the best"—which was debatable—because in those moments, you don't really care. You don't even want what's best. You just want the person you love *back*.

"I can't believe I've really lost her," he sobbed.

"I wish I could help somehow," was all I could think to say. "I'm so sorry."

"It's not your fault honey," he slurred. Yep, definitely drinking. "I never blamed you. You couldn't help it—you were only a baby."

"What?" I asked, unsure if I'd heard him correctly.

There was a pause. "I said there's nothing you can do to help it, baby. Listen, I should get off the phone. I've got to call in sick to work, and I'm in no shape to be talking to you. I'm a big downer right now, and you should be enjoying your trip. I'll talk to you in a few days, okay?"

"Okay," I agreed, further saddened by his attempt to lift his tone and sound more cheerful. I was also reluctant to hang up and leave him to wallow alone. "Bye, Daddy. Love you. Get some sleep."

I turned the phone off and sat for a few more minutes, tilting my head toward the night sky and letting the ocean breeze blow across my tear-streaked cheeks. What a mess my life was. I slipped through the French doors back into the house.

"Oh! You startled me."

One of Nox's servants, a super tall guy all the pod girls called Groot because he never spoke, stood right inside the doorway as if he'd been waiting for me.

Dang. I didn't even realize anyone knew I was outside. But he didn't seem alarmed or even concerned. Maybe he was off duty from being Amalia's lackey tonight.

Groot lifted his palm, presenting me with a folded sheet of white notepaper. I took it and opened it. It was a message signed by Nox.

CHAPTER FOURTEEN
MIDNIGHT SNACK

We need to talk. Please come to my suite. Ewan will lead you.

Okay, so Groot's real name is Ewan. And he was Nox's lackey, not Amalia's. I padded silently after him down the wide, airy hallway, conscious of every closed door we passed. Doors that could open at any moment, exposing me and my destination to anyone who might get up for a drink of water or a midnight snack. Or a late night tryst.

They would certainly assume that was what I was up to. And they'd assume *I* was Nox's midnight snack, since I was being escorted by one of his personal bodyguards. The gleaming polished stone was cool under my bare feet, but the rest of me was growing hotter by the minute. Why would Nox summon me—in the middle of the night—to his suite, the *master* suite, in every possible meaning of the term?

When we reached the huge double doors at the end of the hall, Ewan stepped to the side and took his position opposite the guard who already stood flanking the other side. Neither of them looked at me—they were probably so used to this routine they didn't even blink an eye. Another night, another babe. Or more likely, another hour, another babe.

I raised my hands to push at the doors, but they opened on their own, swinging slowly inward to reveal a glimpse of Nox's private quarters, a place I'd never seen and had tried not to wonder about.

And out stepped Robin, the kissy-face chick from on stage at the club tonight.

Well.

Nox was taking this *spreading it around* thing very seriously. He even kept up the "ruse" inside his private quarters. When she saw me, Robin's eyelids flared and she lifted her chin, turning to look toward the opposite wall of the hallway as she passed me.

Okay. It was like that then. I was actually glad she hadn't said anything. What—were we going to chat like shift workers clocking in and out?

I stood outside the threshold of Nox's suite. How was I supposed to go in there after seeing her walk out? I felt like a piece of fresh meat being delivered to the lion while he was still licking his chops from the last meal.

But then *that* wasn't what I was here for. I was here because I'd been summoned by "the boss" and had to keep up appearances. And Nox had said he wanted to talk to me—about what I wasn't sure. Maybe about the near-assault he'd rescued me from earlier. Considering that, I did owe him at least a civil conversation.

Besides, why should I care what he'd been doing with his evening while I'd been sharing a woozy bus ride with my fellow podsters and talking to my family on the phone? It wasn't my business.

I stepped inside. The doors closed behind me with a click that seemed deafening to my hyper-alert ears in the comparative silence of the room. Nox was nowhere in sight. I did see an enormous fireplace set into a stone wall. Inside it, a fire glowed and colored the surrounding area a soft orange. The sofa and chairs clustered around it were all white, like the luxurious sheepskin rug on the floor in front of it. I snickered. *I'll bet that rug's seen plenty of action.*

Turning away before I could form any further mental images along those lines, I searched the room. Where the heck was he?

"Ryann…" The sound of my name was soft as a whisper, drawn out in a lilting melody that pulled my attention to a pair of balcony doors across the room, standing wide open to the night.

The rush of the surf accompanied his call in perfect harmony. "Ryann…"

I moved toward the music of his voice and the balmy night as he continued to sing my name to me—damn him! Nox knew how his voice affected me, and he was using it against me tonight, though he'd promised not to. Again.

Stepping onto the balcony, I saw him. He stood against the railing looking out, his back to me. I didn't approach him. I said nothing. He already knew I was there, and he knew why I was there better than I did. He'd tell me when he was ready.

Nox turned toward me. His face was shadowed, but I still saw the gleam of his otherworldly hazel eyes. I inhaled sharply and audibly before I could stop myself. I could only hope he hadn't heard it. I hated for him to think the sight of him could affect me like that, even for a moment.

His night-dark hair was haloed by the reflection of the moon on the water behind him. He wore a snug t-shirt and a pair of loose, white, gauzy pants that reached his bare feet. If it had been the first time I'd ever seen him—if I didn't know for certain he was a Dark Elf—I would have thought he was some kind of Heavenly being visiting our planet to weigh the fates of our eternal souls.

At the moment it seemed more likely he had originated from an opposite sort of place. A place where dark beauty like his was born with the sole purpose of tempting someone to forget there was an afterlife at all, any consequences that anything existed beyond the moment at hand.

The ocean breeze lifted my thin white nightgown, alternately billowing it about me like a feather-light sail then plastering it against my figure. The light fabric already left too little to the imagination. I didn't want to think about what it revealed when the warm night wind molded it over my body.

"I'm here." I finally spoke to break the loaded silence.

"Yes you *are*." Nox's heavy-lidded gaze drifted over me. I didn't need a special gift for reading other people's feelings to interpret that look. Either he *hadn't* indulged his sexual appetite with Robin... or he *had*—and it was *that* voracious.

Uncomfortable under his keen scrutiny, I looked away from him and folded my arms across my chest. "So... what did you want?"

"I think I wanted to talk to you about something, but now I can't seem to remember what it was."

"Well, okay then, I guess I'll go back to my room."

I turned to go, but he crossed the balcony and touched my arm.

"No. Stay. I do want to talk to you. How are you feeling? I can't believe you were drugged. I'm so sorry."

"Well. It was my own stupid fault, not yours. And I guess I should thank you for what you did."

His mouth formed a slight close-lipped smile. "There's no need to thank me. Protecting you is my job. I only wish I'd done it a little better, gotten there sooner, before that scumbag had a chance to put his hands and his filthy mouth on you."

I waved a tired hand through the air. "It's okay. I barely remember it—apparently one of the *lovely* after-effects of keta poisoning."

"Well, I remember it. In detail. That guy won't be coming back to the Viper Room anytime soon—I'll tell you that."

We stared at each other silently for a moment. Finally I spoke up. "So, is that what you wanted to talk about? Or is there something else? I've had a really crappy night, and I'm exhausted."

Nox used a finger to tip my head back, giving him a clear view of my face in the light from the bedroom. "You've been crying. Are you sure you weren't injured?"

I twisted my chin out of his light clasp. "No. I talked to my family tonight."

"Oh." He nodded in understanding. "Homesick?"

"Yes, but that's not the main problem." The main problem was that Lad was moving on for good—not that I could discuss it with Nox. "It's my mom. She's—oh never mind—I don't even know why I'm telling you this."

"Because you need a friend right now. And I'm your friend."

Was he? In this whole crazy-big city, he *was* the only person I really knew. I did need a friend, but could I really talk to Nox about something as personal as the death of my parents' marriage? My father being drunk at six a.m.? The end of our family unit once and for all?

Allowing myself to think about it all again was restarting the waterworks. Nox's astute glance told me he'd spotted the telltale moisture in my eyes. I turned away from him and walked to the balcony railing, staring out at the ocean and night sky.

"I think my mom got engaged to her new boyfriend."

Nox's voice behind me was level, full of concern. "That must be strange for you—a big change. I never met him—do you dislike him?"

"No—I mean I haven't met him in person yet, either. We've talked on the phone. He's okay I guess. A bit overeager to be my 'friend,' but he seems like a pretty good guy. It's just… well… this is going to sound stupid, but I guess I was holding out a tiny bit of hope my parents would still get back together…" *And here come the tears.* Wonderful.

I swept my fingers under my eyes, trying to remove the evidence of my wimpiness, but the choked sound of my voice gave me away. "… hope that maybe love really *can* last a lifetime. But now that's just… it's over."

Mom and Daddy. Lad and me. Over. I sniffed and wiped my face again, feeling childish and highly exposed.

Nox didn't respond at first, but when he finally did, his voice was close behind me, soft and gently comforting. "It can, you know. I've seen it."

"Seen what?" I sniffled again, swallowing the uncomfortable lump in my throat.

His hands came to rest lightly on my shoulders. They were large and warm and gentle. "Love. It can last a lifetime—it *does* where I'm from."

As good as his touch felt, it wasn't good to allow it here and now, late at night in his room while I was emotionally torn open. I shrugged off his hands and stepped to the side then turned to face him.

"You mean in Altum, with the Light Elves? I guess so. But you don't believe in that, do you? You're a Dark Elf. You guys do things… differently. You don't bond with one person for life like the Light Elves do."

He crooked an amused grin at me. "Why is it you think you know everything about Dark Elves… and about me?"

I gave him the *oh please* look. "Are you saying Dark Elves have lifetime mates as well?" I shook my head, baffled. "What about all the celebrities hooking up with girls in the fan pods and all the groupies? What about you? If it *was* the same for Dark Elves, you'd have the mark."

I'd learned from Lad that when a bonded Elven pair is forced to part for good, for instance if one of them died, the one left behind would bear a visible mark of mourning for eternity. It was the reason Grandma Neena's hair had gone completely white in her mid-twenties when she was widowed.

"Ryann… are you trying to get me to kiss and tell?" Nox teased.

My face went hot in spite of the cool night air. "No… I uh… assumed you had… been with a lot of girls. I mean, back in Deep River, and now here…"

His grin widened and one eyebrow lifted. "Well, we know what happens when we assume, don't we?"

I rolled my eyes and folded my arms across my chest again. "So you're actually trying to tell me you're not having sex with these girls? With Savannah back in Deep River? With all those groupies? With Robin, whose tonsils you were inspecting with your tongue up on stage tonight, who just walked out of your *bedroom*? I suppose you two just had a nice little fireside chat in here?"

He lifted one dark eyebrow, the side of his mouth quirking in apparent amusement. "Yes. That's what I'm telling you."

I stared at him, incredulous. "What about the blonde from the other night? She was telling everyone about your *amazing* bed."

"Which she saw from across the room. We had some ice cream and played Xbox." He gestured toward a large TV with a gaming setup inside the room.

I stood with my hands on my hips, shaking my head. "Suppose I actually *believed* that horse puckey—why exactly would you have beautiful young girls in your house—in your room *alone* and *not* have sex with them?"

He smiled. "You're in my room alone with me, and I'm not having sex with you."

I dropped my chin and gave him a *get serious* look.

He released a long sigh. "Because I'm only going to bond with someone once, and I have to choose carefully. Dark Elves and Light Elves are different in some regards, Ryann. But not in that one. I'm not saying these other celebrities, like Vallon Foster, are altar boys, that they're *all* playing Xbox and watching movies with their fan pod members like I've been doing. But I can guarantee they're not sleeping with the girls. I assume they're enjoying their fan pods… in a different way."

At my look of obvious confusion he continued. "There are… *certain things* you can do to give and receive pleasure that do not trigger the bond. I'm sure there are plenty of, shall we say *lesser* offenses, going on behind closed doors in their mansions. They never clarify in public how far they've gone or haven't gone with their groupies or any of the women they meet and invite home. People assume they're having orgies or one night stands, and they don't correct those assumptions."

"And the pod members themselves can't set the record straight because they're glamoured."

"Exactly."

"So then, these girls *think* they're having sex with celebrities they've never actually slept with?"

"Maybe. There's no way they could really know the difference—glamour is like the ultimate roofie—the girls have no reliable memory of what happened the night before. For instance, a girl I bring in here only knows she was with me. Her imagination fills in the blanks. She might assume we've had sex and probably couldn't tell for sure… unless the girl was a virgin *herself.*"

Unless the girl was a virgin herself. Something about the phrase grabbed my attention and was now bouncing around in my brain.

"Nox—you're saying *you're* a… virgin?"

"Well, I didn't *say* it…"

But his eyes were saying it. The vulnerable set of his mouth was saying it. And common sense was saying it.

If the rule for Dark Elves and Light Elves really was the same… then Nox would have been bound to the first girl he'd slept with. And as soon as he'd broken the bond by sleeping with another girl, his hair would have gone pure white overnight. He had to be telling the truth.

I went back into his suite and stopped in front of the fireplace, pondering the absurdity. The flames danced as if they were laughing at the very idea of it. Nox Knight. High School Hero. Rock God. Virgin.

The possibility had never crossed my mind. Now I couldn't get it *out* of my mind. What did this mean? What about those times when we had kissed and things had gotten super-hot super-fast?

Unlike Lad, who'd always stopped us just as things were getting good, Nox had never put on the brakes, never even downshifted into less intense making out. As far as I could tell, he'd been pressing the gas pedal to the floor, trying to push things toward can't-turn-back-now territory with me. But why?

He came up behind me on the furry rug, not touching me, but standing very close. "Can I ask you a question?"

I turned to face him. The reflection of the fireplace in his hazel eyes made him look like the Devil I'd believed he was until a few moments ago. It was hard to shake that impression of him so quickly.

"What?"

"How did you feel when you saw me going off after supper with the blonde the other night? And when you saw me kiss Robin up on stage tonight?" He paused. "Were you jealous?"

The words "of course not" came out of my mouth. Unfortunately, the word *Yes* sprang into my mind loud and clear, and I was with one of only two guys I knew in the world who could hear what I was saying, even when I didn't say it aloud.

A satisfied grin spread across his face. "You were."

"I didn't say that."

"Yes you did. You said it in the Elven way. And as we both know, it's impossible to lie that way."

Embarrassed and feeling somewhat violated by his mind-reading, I spun away from him again, staring into the flames as if they held the secret to life.

I was jealous, too.

The thought came to me as clearly as if Nox had spoken it aloud. I squeezed my eyes tightly shut and took a deep breath. Oh no. What was happening here?

He swept my hair to one side, and his large hands settled on my upper arms. His voice was soft and low as he spoke close to my ear.

"I was. That's why I jumped off stage and followed you two out of the club. I didn't realize at the time he'd drugged you—I just couldn't stand to see you going off with some other guy. At first I thought you'd jumped into a cab with him, and I was about to—I don't know—steal a car or something and go looking for you. Then I heard your scream from around the side of the building. When I saw him pinning you up against the wall with his filthy mouth on your throat…"

Now Nox brushed my hair to the other side, and I realized he was studying my neck, looking for signs of damage. I knew when he spotted the hickey because his low growl filled my ear. He didn't say anything about it directly, though. Instead, he lowered his face until his lips barely came into contact with the ugly bruised spot, brushing it with the lightest of pressure.

"You smell good," he whispered against my sensitive skin, his hot breath making me shiver, even though I was warm in the radiant heat of the fireplace. "So sweet. I like your shower gel—is it vanilla?"

I nodded, unable to answer him and unable to move. Unable to breathe. A fire had started in my belly that made the blaze in the fireplace look like a matchstick. *This is bad.* Maybe Nox had the glamour of super-strong persuasion in addition to music? But no, I feared it was something much worse. Lad had mentioned some Elves had sexual glamour.

Wouldn't that just make the most perfect rock star? A hot Elven guitar player and lead singer with the double-whammy of musical and sexual glamour? He'd be unstoppable. He'd own the world. He'd certainly own any girl he set his mind to having.

And, at the moment, his mind seemed to be set on me.

Chapter Fifteen
First Loves

Again, his lips brushed my neck, this time with more pressure. I shivered, and his large, warm hands coasted up and down my upper arms, soothing away the chill bumps. Nox kissed a path down to my shoulder then back up to the sensitive spot behind my ear.

All the while I stood perfectly still, my chest rising and falling rapidly and my heart pounding wildly, while the rest of me felt incapable of movement.

Was this sexual glamour? Or was it just Nox? Maybe it was a rebound reaction to the news about Lad and Vancia tonight. Maybe it was the natural culmination of weeks of being in each other's presence in a strange situation full of pressures and unknown threats. Mutual attraction to be sure. Mutual loneliness as well?

Whatever it was, it was filling my belly with warmth, injecting my limbs with the urge to turn around and lift my arms to him, wrap them around his neck and kiss him back.

Perhaps sensing my reaction or growing impatient with my lack of response, Nox dropped his hands to my waist and turned my body, bringing us face-to-face. "Ryann," he whispered.

I thought he was about to ask permission to kiss me.

He didn't.

That wasn't Nox's style. He brought a hand up to cup my jaw and the side of my neck and pulled me in for his mouth to claim, taking the kiss he wanted. And oh how he kissed. He licked and sucked and pulled at my lips, tilting his head to the side, angled even closer. The scent of his skin filled my nostrils, the soft sound of his urgent breathing sent my pulse into erratic rhythms.

Pulling away slightly, Nox spoke against my mouth. "God, Ryann, you taste so good, you feel so good to me. I want you so much."

I nodded, wanting him, too. I couldn't deny it. He was so beautiful, so intoxicating. His touch was maddening, and the way he kissed me made me feel desired, wanted. Lad no longer wanted me, but someone did. And that someone was right here, staring into my eyes.

Nox must have read my nod as some sort of agreement because he scooped me into his arms and carried me toward the bed, which as advertised, was enormous. The out-of-body sense of peace and rightness lifted a fraction, allowing a sliver of rationality to slip in, followed by a thrill of alarm.

What are we doing? This is getting serious.

Nox set me gently in the center of his bed then backed away as if admiring the sight of me there. A dreamy smile spread across his face, and his eyelids went heavy as he took me in with an unmistakable look of hunger.

"Look at you," he whispered and blew out a long, slow breath. He lifted the bottom of his shirt and pulled it over his head in one movement, letting it fall to the floor.

Oh help. His body was amazing. What was I going to do? On one hand, I was right where I wanted to be. My heart was doing cartwheels, cheered on by every hormone in my body. But as he crawled across the bed toward me, the panicky feeling grew.

If he kissed me again and started touching me, I might not have the willpower to stop where it would lead. And if I didn't, things were going to get *very* permanent between us *very* fast. As in tonight. At least it would be permanent on his end. He was Elven, and if what he'd said was the truth, sex was a one-person-for-life thing, for Light and Dark Elves alike.

"We can't," I managed to choke out, just as he reached me.

The hand Nox was sliding around my waist stopped. "Can't what?" Now the fingers resumed their seductive stroking, gliding over my wispy nightgown to my hip, thigh, down to my knee and pushing underneath so his palm made breathtaking, fire-sparking contact with my skin as he kissed my neck and collarbone and dipped his head lower.

Ohgodohgodohgod I knew I had to say it fast, or it was never going to be said. Pressing my palms against the mattress beneath me, I scooted myself away from him.

"We can't make love," my mouth said as my body ached to do exactly that. I could already tell how incredible it would feel to be under his big body, his weight and hard muscles over me.

The lust-soaked haze cleared a little from Nox's face. "Why not?"

"Because... we can't. We're not thinking straight. We can't get distracted. There are consequences. There are other people involved here."

I was referring to Emmy and our mission to rescue her from the other fan pod, but based on Nox's reaction, his mind had gone to an entirely different place.

He stopped trying to touch me and raised up onto his knees, the muscles in his chest and arms contracting tightly as his hands fisted. "It's Lad, isn't it? It's always *him*. You're still hung up on him." He rolled off the bed and stalked away a few feet.

"No, that's not it," I said to his back. "I realize... it's over between Lad and me. We won't ever be together."

Nox spun back around to face me. "But you *wish* you could be with him." His face was a canvas of barely controlled pain. "Even when you're kissing me and responding to my touch, you're still thinking of him." He balled his fists, blinking rapidly.

My heart lurched toward him. It killed me to see him hurting like this. I slid off the edge of the mattress and went to him, reaching out. He took a step back in a halfhearted attempt to evade me, but I kept going and placed my hands against the hot skin of his abdomen.

Looking up into his face, I told him honestly. "That's not true. I wasn't thinking of him when we kissed. Or when we were in the bed. But I can't *not* think of Emmy. We *have* to think of her. We're not here on vacation. And even though what I said was true—Lad and I are over—I'm also not sure I'm ready to move on yet."

"Because you're still in love with him?"

"Well... no... I don't know. You can't really be 'in love' alone, I guess. And feeling that way only hurts me when he doesn't feel the same. I don't *want* to love him anymore. I mean—he doesn't even know where I am or what's happening to me—maybe he doesn't even care. So I shouldn't care. But he *was* my first love, and I'll probably always feel something for him—you know how it is."

He stared at me. I stared back.

"Haven't you ever been in love?"

He held my gaze, flags of color rising in his face. "Hmmm." He laughed uncomfortably and then looked away, rubbing his forehead.

Suddenly, I was way more interested in the answer than I had been before. I could tell by his body language there had indeed been someone, and now my curiosity burned. Who was she? This girl who'd captured the heart of the guy everyone wanted?

"You have, haven't you?" I took a step toward him. "Nox, come on. I'm spilling my guts out here. Tell me you know what I'm talking about. Or am I the only idiot in the room?"

His eyes came back to me. "No. I'm *definitely* an idiot."

I leaned toward him and bumped him gently with my shoulder. "So... give it up. Who was she?"

Nox looked down into my face. Instead of answering, he slid an arm around my waist and pulled me tighter against him. "I don't want to talk about that," he whispered, and then his mouth was on mine.

The kiss was deep, probing, more emotional than any other kiss we'd shared. As our tongues moved together, it was if he was pulling at my soul, trying to convince me of some truth yet unspoken.

After a minute I started to break the contact, but his grip on me tightened and the sensuous assault kicked into a higher gear. And Nox began humming deep in his throat, calling on the maddening musical glamour I was powerless to resist.

I felt myself teetering at the edge of a cliff. Scrambling for a desperate toehold, I slapped hard at his bare arm.

He lifted his head, looking mesmerized himself. "What was that for?"

"I've told you not to do that to me—no singing."

"I'm sorry—it just starts happening when I'm happy. And I wanted you to enjoy—"

"I *know* what you wanted. But Nox, even if I believed it was a good idea for us, we *can't*. Use your head. You have to think about what *that*..." I pointed to his rumpled bed. "…would mean for you and your future. You weren't handing me a line with the virginity thing, were you?"

"No." He sighed and ran a hand through the top of his hair in a frustrated gesture. "It's unfortunately very, very true."

"So then you have to be really careful. You can't just go bonding yourself to some random human girl because you're… horny."

Now he let out a shocked laugh. "I can't believe you said the word 'horny.' And you're *not* some random human. Besides, you're part Elven, remember."

"Yes, but only a quarter, and there's no guarantee I'll have a lifespan any longer than a regular human. You're immortal. If you were to get carried away and bond yourself to me, and then we went our separate ways or I died, you'd carry the mark forever."

"Ryann, you're acting like I haven't considered any of this. I'm not a fourteen year old following his junk around wherever it leads. I'm fully aware of the potential consequences every time we're alone together."

"Oh. So… why do you even start making out with me then?"

Nox dropped his chin and leveled me with the universal expression for *Really?*

Well, of course I understood *that* motivation. But was he so sure of his ability to stop? Then it occurred to me— maybe he never intended to go *all* the way.

"Is it what you were talking about earlier? What the other Dark Elves do? You want to do the *other things* you referred to that don't bond you to someone for life?"

My face heated at the visions rushing through my imagination—acts that would bring pleasure but not result in a permanent bond. My mental repertoire was small, no doubt, compared to the vast array of things a man and woman could do together, but it was still blush-inducing.

Nox grinned now, apparently amused by my naiveté. "Of course, I wouldn't *mind* doing those *other things*... with you. But I'm not afraid of bonding with you. You should know that by now."

"I don't understand you." I shook my head at him in wonder.

"No. You don't. But since you've already informed me we *won't* be making love, then there's no need for me to get into all my reasons for wanting to."

"Oh." And now I was feeling strangely let down. "So... I guess this is where we play Xbox?" I gave a nervous giggle.

"If you want." Nox took my hand and led me to the white sectional sofa in front of the fireplace. He pulled me down to sit beside him. "Or... we could talk about what I called you here to tell you in the first place. I've got a lead on Emmy."

"What?" I bounced up off the sofa again. "Why didn't you say that in the first place?"

"Well there was a beautiful girl in my room in a semi-transparent nightgown, and my memory was temporarily impaired."

Glancing down at my chest, I crossed my arms in front of it and sat back down. "So what's the lead?"

"Vallon Foster was at the Viper Room last night—did you see him?"

"No. I guess I should've been studying Emmy's magazines. Some of the girls were saying there were several actors and musicians there, but it was dark, and I didn't really recognize anyone famous."

"Well, he was there, sitting in Booth Four with the booking manager. I had my people invite him to the show. We spoke afterward." He raised one eyebrow. "We've been invited to a party."

I sat even straighter. "We?"

"Me and my fan pod. It's this weekend at his compound on Carbon Beach."

"Oh my God! This is amazing, Nox. This is our chance to find Emmy. She'll be there, right? If he told you to bring your fan pod, he'll bring his, right?"

"I'm pretty sure. That seems to be how it works. It's... how should I put this... part of the entertainment?"

I stilled. "What do you mean?" We wouldn't be expected to put on some sort of sordid floor show for our "masters" would we?

"Don't worry—I'll make sure you're not a part of it. It's sort of a game, like... like trading cards... only with girls." He glanced up at me from under his brows as if expecting a slap.

My stomach bottomed out and went cold. "You mean the Dark Elves *trade* girls from fan pod to fan pod?"

"Apparently. At least that's what Alfred hinted at. I'm sure I'll get a great education by spending some time with Vallon. He's got the largest fan pod and has been at it the longest."

"Well, I can't wait to meet *him*," I said, sarcasm coloring the words.

"I don't *want* you to meet him. But it is our best chance of finding Emmy."

"Great. What should I wear?" Of course it didn't matter. I'd be happy to show up in my yoga pants and a ratty t-shirt. All I cared about was getting Emmy back. And it was finally going to happen.

Chapter Sixteen
The Movie Star

If the TV station visit and Viper Room show had caused a frenzy among my fellow fan podders, then the announcement of a star-studded Hollywood party had incited absolute pandemonium. Some of the girls were actually throwing up in our dorm before we boarded the bus for Vallon's beach house.

All of us wore swanky evening wear provided by Amalia. I had no idea where she'd gotten it or how she'd nailed all our dress and shoe sizes, but apparently it was important for us to look occasion-appropriate because all of it bore designer labels.

Between the Laboutins and the Chanel, we were wearing a collective fortune. *Oh my gosh.* Were those designers Elven, too?

I'd never worn anything that hadn't been purchased at a discount store or run-of-the-mill department store, but the sparkly dress wasn't what excited me about the evening. After all these weeks, all the worry, I was about to see Emmy again.

As we boarded the bus, I tried to prepare myself that she might have changed. She might look different, act different. She might not even recognize me if she'd been glamoured thoroughly enough. It didn't matter. I'd finally know where she was and *how* she was and could begin the work of getting her back home safely.

The bus came to a stop on the Pacific Coast Highway outside the mansion, and Amalia stood to give us instructions. "You are here to represent Nox and serve his interests, to be seen and not heard. If someone speaks to you, you may converse with them, but you are *not* to approach any celebrities. They may choose to approach you, even invite you to an event. Only then are you allowed to interact with them.

We entered the ultra-modern beach home in a parade of tanned skin and stilettoes. And fit right in. It was bizarre to be surrounded by so much beauty—like I'd stepped into a magazine or a CW primetime show.

The girls with me dispersed, moving through the crowd, each no doubt hoping some celebrity would spot her and strike up a conversation. I shuddered at the knowledge of what was really going on here—the real reason the Dark Elves had brought along their fan pods— and began a search of the room.

Every few minutes, a servant would stop with a tray, offering me an appetizer, a sparkling drink. I refused it all.

I wasn't here to have a good time. I was here for one reason only—to find Emmy.

She didn't seem to be on the first floor, so I climbed the beautiful open staircase to the next floor and walked through the rooms, scanning in every direction. I hadn't seen Nox yet, though I knew he was here somewhere because I'd overheard some girls from another pod chattering and giggling over spotting him.

She's not here. Moving on.

I climbed the staircase to the third floor where a DJ was playing retro Disco music inside at the bar, much to the delight of the party-goers who filled the dance floor. Squeezing past them, I made my way to the open-air roof deck. There was music out here, too, but not as loud, allowing for conversation among the groups of people enjoying the night air, sea breeze, and moonlit ocean view.

Walking the perimeter of the large deck, I spotted someone who made my heart pound like the drumbeat from the alternative band playing in the corner. Not Emmy—but the next best thing. The one person who knew for sure where she'd been the past two weeks.

He was leaning against the deck railing, his tall, perfectly sculpted form framed by a backdrop of stars over the Malibu beach, and naturally, surrounded by a crowd of adoring teenage girls and twenty-something women.

Adrenaline surged through my veins like the surf I could hear in the background. Finally, after everything I'd gone through to get here, I was so close to finding her.

Preparing to charge Vallon Foster—huge Elven bodyguards be damned—I planned to demand Emmy's whereabouts and immediate release. A strong hand gripped my shoulder and slid down to my waist. I was pulled back against the solid warmth of a large male body.

"Calm down, Ryann," the smooth familiar voice murmured at my ear. "And let me handle this."

With considerable effort, I reeled in my emotions and pasted on a smile. We approached the movie star together, hand in hand.

"Sweetheart, I'd like you to meet my good friend, Vallon Foster." The voice of the beautiful guy beside me was comforting, full of loving assurance.

I forced myself to appear something less-than-hostile as Nox introduced me.

"Vallon, this is Ryann… the newest member of my fan pod."

The movie star looked different in person, younger and more handsome, if that were possible. He wore a silvery gray suit with a black shirt underneath, unbuttoned nearly to the center of his chest. His dark hair was slicked back from his tanned face, revealing the ice blue eyes so many moviegoers (and co-stars) had fallen in love with. There was no denying it. He was a beautiful man.

Vallon seemed to appreciate my appearance as well. Either that, or he stared lewdly at every young girl who crossed his path—I hadn't been around him long enough to know yet.

His eyes browsed my body, stopping at the parts he found most interesting, then continuing their perusal. Up and down. Down and then back up. When his gaze finally landed on my face, his lips spread into the most predatory smile I'd ever seen... like a crocodile oh-so-politely introducing himself to a small animal shivering on the shoreline.

"Well, well, Nox. Looks like you're off to a good start with your first crop of girls. I'll have to talk to Alfred, though—he must be sending me the second class choices if *this* is what he's sending you—and on your maiden voyage, too. Lucky boy."

Nox cleared his throat and looked at his feet, twisting his lips before answering tightly. "Thank you."

Vallon lifted a hand to the side in a lazy gesture. "Feel free to look around and take whatever you'd like from my stable. You'll find I'm very generous with my friends." Giving me another interested glance he turned back to Nox. "I hope *you* feel the same?"

"Oh, of course. But since I got my girls only a few days ago—I'll probably just hang on to what I've got for now. I don't even know all their names yet."

Apparently that amused Vallon. He burst into laughter and slapped his leg. "Oh—that is priceless. I love the newbies. God, I haven't known the names of one of mine for ages now. It hardly matters."

Nox's face reddened. "Well, I'm still learning the rules, I guess."

"Stick with me my boy—I'll be happy to show you how it's done. So where did this sweet plum come from?"

He was talking about me as if I wasn't there. My blood started boiling—I'd been in his presence exactly three minutes, and I hated him. I wasn't a piece of meat, and I *did* have a name. So did Emmy—not that he would know it.

"I'm from Mississippi," I snapped, looking directly at him.

He laughed out loud again. "Oh my. A feisty personality to go with the lovely body and face. You are *precisely* my favorite flavor, my little Southern Belle." His eyes turned to Nox again. "Actually, I had one from Mississippi myself. Cute thing—outrageous accent. She was quite delicious except for the glasses."

My heart seized—he was talking about Emmy. And he'd said he *had* her. What did that mean? Was she not with him anymore? Had he sent her home? Was she okay?

I couldn't ask about Emmy myself—it would tip Vallon off to my un-glamoured condition. But I turned and looked at Nox, willing him to ask. In fact, I was fairly screaming it inside my head.

He must have gotten the message because he repeated my silent question out loud. "Where's she tonight? I'd like to check her out. I have a thing for the Southern ones, too."

Vallon flipped his manicured fingers in a bored gesture. "Well, she was fun for a while, but they all get old rather quickly, you know? No, I guess you don't—but you will. I traded her to Reggie."

"Reggie Dillon, the Tremors' quarterback?" Nox asked.

"Yes, have you met him yet?"

"Not yet—I haven't been in town very long."

"Oh, you'll like him. He's *lots* of fun. And he has excellent taste in fine young things. Make sure you get an introduction and check out his stable." Vallon browsed my body again, cataloguing my individual attributes from head to toe. "So... how would *you* feel about making a trade tonight? One of my girls for this one? Any one you want—take two in fact." He did everything short of licking his lips in anticipation.

Nox's grip on my hand tightened painfully. I tried not to wince—it wouldn't do to alert Vallon to my companion's spontaneous reaction.

His voice betrayed nothing as he emulated Vallon's blasé tone. "Well... that's a nice offer. But I haven't had a chance to sample this one yet. Listen, I see someone over there Alfred wanted me to meet—I'm going to say hi. Great party. Come on, Ryann."

"Keep it in mind—whenever you're done with her," Vallon yelled to our backs as Nox nearly dragged me across the rooftop toward the far end of the bar.

"Who are we going to see?" I asked, running to keep up with his hard-digging stride.

"Anyone but that asshole," Nox growled. "I didn't want you spending another second with him."

His protective tone sent a flutter of nerves through my midsection. "Yeah—he was pretty horrible. I don't even want to think about what he did to Emmy—or made her do before he got rid of her."

Nox pulled me into an alcove between the bar and a potted tree. "You're better off *not* thinking about it. At least we know where she is now."

"Yes—and we know how to get her back."

He shook his head. "I haven't gotten quite that far yet. What do you mean?"

"Well, you'll have to trade me, of course."

He stiffened, his already tense facial muscles tightening further. "What? Absolutely not! You saw what Vallon's like. Reggie could be worse."

"I doubt anyone could be worse than Vallon." I laughed.

Nox's frown said he didn't find any humor in the situation. "Well, it doesn't matter. I'm *not* trading you for Emmy. What good would it do, anyway? Then she'd be free, and you'd be trapped."

"But I wouldn't be. Since I won't be glamoured, I'd be able to escape."

Noticing a couple looking at us, Nox spun me around and pulled me further into the dark alcove. In a lowered voice he said, "How do you know you won't be susceptible to Reggie's glamour? You might be. You've never even met him."

"Well, he's an athlete, not a musician. Chances are if I'm susceptible to musical glamour, I'm resistant to other kinds, right? Lad wasn't able to glamour me at all."

Nox's eyebrows lifted at this news, and a pleased half-smile developed before he mastered it and got serious again. "What if Reggie won't trade Emmy? He only just got her."

"Then you could trade me for another girl in his fan pod—I could get in there with Emmy and maybe *un*-brainwash her or something. We could escape together. Maybe I could even help a few of the other girls he has there."

Nox shook his head, the stubborn frown returning. "No way, Ryann. I like this plan less and less all the time."

Grabbing his forearm, I squeezed it, trying to make him see reason. "This is our best chance to find Emmy. If I don't do this, what are we even here for? I might as well go home. Oh my God, is that Chris Hemsworth?"

He glanced over at the tall, muscular movie star who'd stepped onto the roof deck with his stunning model wife. "Yeah, I met him at the Assemblage ten years ago—he's from the Australian clan."

"Right." I nodded. "I probably should've guessed *that* one."

CHAPTER SEVENTEEN
TRUTH OR DARE

Nox asked me to meet him on the pool deck later that night, after everyone had gone to bed. He was already outside when I opened the back door.

"All right," he said with a sigh.

I beamed at him. "You'll arrange something with Reggie?"

"The team's got training camp this week—it's closed to the public, but I can get us in. I'm *not* promising to arrange a trade. We'll just *meet* him, check him out personally. Maybe we'll even see Emmy there—I understand the pods are encouraged to be there. But I've got a condition."

"What is it?"

"If I get a bad feeling about him, we're walking away."

"But—"

He held up a silencing hand. "We will walk *away*. And… I want you to work on your nonverbal communication."

I blew out an impatient breath. "Why?"

"Because I'll feel better if we can communicate that way. You've heard me a time or two, and I've heard you, but you've got a long way to go before you're actually proficient. I sent you messages a few times during the party tonight, and you didn't seem aware of them. I need to be sure you can hear me *every* time, in case I need to give you some sort of warning or instruction for your own safety. Or in case we get separated. Plus, it'd be a great way to get around my guard dog when we're here at home."

"Guard dog?"

He hooked a thumb toward the house. "Amalia."

I laughed at his description of her. "So what's her deal, anyway?"

He shrugged and shook his head. "Alfred sent her over with the first group of fan pod members—called her a 'house manager.' She seems more like a spy to me, though."

"I thought the same thing. A spy for whom, though?"

"The Dark Council, I guess."

"Is there anyone here you trust completely? Anyone who's loyal to you?"

"Yes. Ewan, the one who brought you the note last night. He's been with me since I first got out to California. He actually worked for my parents when I was a kid. I re-hired him first thing when I set up a residence here."

"That's nice. Also, it's weird. It's hard for me to get used to the fact that someone you knew as a child could look almost as young as we are."

"Yeah, it must be strange to a human. I'm used to it."

"So… what kind of intel do you think your house spy is here to gather?"

"Probably checking to see if I'm with the Dark Elven program. I mean, to them, my past is a mystery. I told Alfred as little as I could get away with. But he knows I spent the past five years in Mississippi—Light Elf territory. He might be worried I interacted with them too much, that I developed sympathies with the Light Kingdom or something."

"So which side *are* you on?"

He leaned back on his hands and stared up at the starry sky. "Hmmm… I'm not sure I'm on any side. I came to understand the Light Elves very well while I lived in Altum. And I love some of them deeply. But of course, I was born a Dark Elf and lived among them the first twelve years of my life. I feel loyal to that side. I wish there weren't two sides, honestly, but that's like saying you wish there weren't different denominations of churches or different political parties. People will always disagree."

"True. I guess you have to get to know them better before you can really decide. Have you figured out what the fan pods are for yet?"

"I think so. I mean, clearly it's about winning the love and loyalty of humans—as many as possible and getting them as deeply invested as possible. If we have influential young people working to create new fans for us, then we have a stronger following. I'm not sure how much Lad told you about our histories, but Elves used to be the rulers of Earth. Humans following us and serving our needs was the natural order of things, and from what I gather, the Dark Elves want things to go back to the way they were. Fan pods seem to be one step in the plan toward the ultimate goal."

"Which is?"

"To eventually be able to 'come out of the closet' and be open about who and what we are, to stop hiding, stop fearing human discovery. The Dark Elven leaders believe the only way we'll be safe in doing that is if the humans are under our power. You outnumber us tremendously."

"I remember Lad telling me that. You know, I understand about them wanting to have freedom to be who they are and come and go as they please without having to hide their identities, but I can't say I'm crazy about the whole plan for world domination."

Nox wrinkled his nose and nodded. "Yeah. I'm not too comfortable with the whole idea myself. But it's hard. I mean, I have to accept who I am, right? My parents were Dark Elves, and they weren't bad people."

"But they died under mysterious circumstances. Isn't that what you said?"

"Yeah. So?"

"Well, think about it. Maybe your parents, who were very influential, *weren't* on board with the Dark Council's plans. Maybe they were causing trouble, stirring up doubt among other Elves or something. Maybe that's why they were killed. Maybe that's why your mom escaped in the middle of the night and put you in the heart of the Light Elves' Kingdom—the furthest place from the Dark Council's hands."

He blinked and jerked his head back as if he'd been slapped. "Whoa. You may be right." Rubbing his face with one hand, he went on. "If you are, then I've done the stupidest thing possible by coming back here and immersing myself in the Dark Elven world again. Maybe that was why Ivar was so angry with me when he learned I'd been sneaking off to California. I thought he was trying to boss me around—control me." He ran a hand through his hair. "Man, I sound like a pouty teenager, don't I?"

I laughed and held my fingers up an inch apart. "Teensy bit."

"Even more reason we need you to get up to speed on your Elven communication. You and I..." He gestured between our bodies "...we're the only people we can truly count on out here. We might need to send an emergency message at some point."

"Okay, so how do we do it?"

He appeared to think for a minute, staring out at the rolling sea. "How about a game of Truth or Dare?"

A trill of alarm went through my body. I'd always hated that game at middle school parties. It was probably even more dangerous and potentially embarrassing now. "How about 'I Spy' instead?"

He grinned. "No. We're going to play Truth or Dare. That—or no meeting with Reggie."

"Fine. Who's going first?" I grumbled.

"You go, since you're the weak link here."

"Hey." I smacked his arm. "All right. You're right. Okay… let me see…" I focused my thoughts, forming a message for Nox. The question I'd asked him the other night in his suite—the one he'd refused to answer—came immediately to mind. I knew it would be impossible for him to lie to me when we were speaking mind-to-mind.

Truth or dare—who was your first love?

He narrowed his eyes and smirked.

Dare.

I laughed out loud. I was winning this game already. Hmm… what was something I could make him do that he'd hate? Aha. Thinking I'd send him into the ocean for a chilly nighttime swim, I formulated a command and pushed the mental send button.

Take off your shirt.

And then immediately regretted it. He wasn't aware of the context of my words, only that I was suggesting he undress.

His eyes flared as he looked at me. And then he got to his feet and slowly peeled his shirt off, grasping the bottom and pulling the garment over his head, staring at me steadily through the process.

As it dropped to the deck he gave me a sexy smile. "How'd I do?"

I got to my feet and cleared my throat. "Um, yeah. That was good. I was thinking I'd make you run into the ocean, but I didn't want you to have to do it in your clothes. Sorry. You can put it back on now."

"It's not hypnosis, Ryann. You can't *make* me do anything I don't want to do. And I think I'll leave it off. Okay, my turn."

Nox stared deeply into my eyes. I couldn't hear anything at first and I was starting to get uncomfortable. Was I failing the experiment already? And then I realized he was taking his time coming up with a question for me. I wasn't really worried about what he'd ask—I had nothing to hide.

Who's a better kisser? Me... or Lad?

Dang it. I didn't want to talk about that. And I couldn't lie to him—not communicating this way. Only one thing I could say.

Dare.

You got it. Take off your *clothes now.* When my eyes widened to the size of teacups, he laughed. *Just kidding. Get up and walk to the stairs, go down them, and stop at the edge of the water.*

I'd heard him, even over the sound of my heartbeat pounding in my ears. Crossing the deck, I descended the stairs and walked across the beach, stopping as my toes reached the lapping surf. *Ohmigod the water's cold!*

He laughed. *Excellent, now—*

Hold on, mister. Your turn is over. It's my turn now. Hmmm... He wanted to play hardball? I could ask questions that made him squirm, too.

Who's the prettiest girl in your fan pod?

Easy. You.

No—that's not a legitimate answer. Give me another name.

I can't remember any of their names.

Okay then—it's a dare. Do a cartwheel in the sand.

"Ryann..." he complained aloud.

No whining. Either do a cartwheel or run into the ocean. And if you're wondering... the water's effing cold... beware of shrinkage.

Well, since I haven't done a cartwheel since I was about eight and would probably pull a muscle...

Nox unbuttoned his shorts and let them drop to the sand around his feet. Underneath he wore boxer briefs, which he began to inch down his hips.

Heart sputtering, I spun around to face the opposite way. "What are you doing?" I screeched, completely forgetting we were supposed to communicate without sound.

Accepting your dare. And be ready... because my turn is coming up next.

The sound of splashing and a whoosh of expelled air was followed by a hearty male laugh. "Damn this *is* cold!"

When I turned to search the water, I could see the top of his head and his face glowing pale in the lights from the house shining across the dark waves.

I'm going to make you pay for that one, he threatened silently. *Truth or Dare—I've never been glamoured, and I'm curious. What goes through your mind when you hear me sing?*

I glared at him. He had stacked the deck. He was purposely asking me questions he knew I wouldn't answer. *Dare*, I muttered in my mind.

His smile gleamed. *Come on in, baby, the water's fine.*

I'm not taking off my clothes, I insisted.

I didn't say anything about your clothes this time. Keep them or lose them—but I'd hate to hear what Amalia will have to say if she finds out you ruined a twenty thousand dollar Prada dress with salt water.

Dang! Did it really cost that much? Nox—give me a different dare. I couldn't wear a bra under this gown.

His white teeth glowed against the darkness of the night sky and the deep blue ocean around him. He shrugged. *Not my problem. But if you can't follow the rules of a simple game, maybe you're not ready to tangle with Reggie Dillon.*

"Fine," I muttered. Then without speaking, I added, *But close your eyes until I get into the water.*

He laughed and held a hand over the top half of his face.

I slipped one strap off my shoulder, then another, before clamping my arm across my breasts and letting the gown fall. Shooting a glance at Nox, I confirmed he still had his hand across his eyes. Wearing only my panties now, I tiptoed into the water, making small noises of complaint the whole way and dreading each moment the next inch of bare skin would contact the chilly water.

It's easier if you go under all at once.

My gaze flew to Nox, who was now peeking at me from between his spread fingers. *Hey! You're not supposed to be looking until I got all the way under.*

How was I supposed to know when *you got all the way under unless I peeked?*

Because I was going to tell you idiot. Oh—you are such a cheater. You were peeking the whole time, weren't you?

"No," he said aloud.

I was relieved until it hit me. "Hey—wait a minute—you answered me out loud on that one! I want to hear you answer the Elven way."

"Maybe I did," he said with a rascally grin. "Maybe you just didn't hear it. Maybe you need to work on your skills some more." And he dived under the water, disappearing from sight.

Suddenly there was a hard jerk on my ankle and I went under as well. Immediately, the grip around my leg was released and I popped to the surface, spitting salt water and highly perturbed.

"You are completely untrustworthy, you know that?"

"Maybe. But I'm also your best protection against piranhas."

"Piranhas? There aren't any piranhas here—they're tropical fish, and these waters are definitely not tropical."

"You haven't heard of the rare Pacific piranhas? Oh, they're notorious on California beaches. They don't bite though—they tickle." As he spoke the last word, Nox made contact with my ribcage and began tickling me mercilessly.

Shrieking and leaping away from him, I tried to swim for shore with my one free arm, but Nox caught me around the waist and pulled me back to deeper waters—over my head, actually.

I don't like this. I didn't like how dark it was out here away from the house lights. I didn't like how warm and alluring his hot skin felt against mine. It made me want to cling to him instead of push him away as I should.

I struggled against his grip again, and in my struggle, succeeded in dunking myself, swallowing a nasty gulp of briny water in the process. Strong hands hooked underneath my armpits and lifted me. I coughed and spat, trying to expel the ocean from my mouth and lungs.

"I'm sorry," Nox said. "I was just playing—didn't mean to drown you there."

As I continued to cough, my body began shuddering with cold. The playful fun of the moment had passed.

"Aww... I am such an idiot," Nox said and pulled me against his chest, patting my back to help me get the remaining water out.

He must have been standing on the bottom because his body didn't sway with the current like mine did. In fact he was rock solid. In every definition of the word.

My cold skin pressed against him, my softness against his hardness, and the warmth of him was absolutely heavenly. I needed to move away, put some distance between our bodies, but I couldn't do it. Not yet.

My coughing subsided, replaced by long, even breaths. The hard pats on my back became firm strokes and then gentle caresses as both of us settled into the embrace.

I'm topless. With a guy. I'm topless with a guy. With Nox. At least he couldn't see anything, but as chilled as I was, and being shirtless himself, Nox could certainly *feel* things. A deep groan from his chest told me he was very much enjoying what he felt.

I lifted my body away from him, keeping my forehead against his chest and hopefully blocking his view. "Let's go in. I need to dry off and w-warm up."

"Yes." His grip on me relaxed, but he didn't let go entirely. "Ryann…" He stared down at me, not sending me any messages with his mind, but when I glanced up at them, his eyes were definitely communicating something. Desire.

I tore my own gaze away. "We should go in," I repeated, though I wasn't feeling nearly as cold as I had before.

We swam to shore, and as we reached shallow water, I slowed, staying submerged to my shoulders. "Okay, you go on ahead. I'll be inside in a minute."

"What? No. I'm not leaving you out here. Let me run up to the deck and get you a towel."

"Please Nox. Just go."

"No way."

I sighed. "Fine. I'll go first then. I don't trust you not to look when you're on your way back." And I walked around him, marching across the sand and up the stairs with my arms clamped across my chest. I was pretty sure he watched me the whole way, but at least all he was getting was a view of my back. And my bottom, though my black panties were no skimpier than the bikini bottoms all the girls had worn earlier.

Besides, he'd seen plenty of scantily clad female derrieres in his time. I had no doubt of that. Could mine really be any more interesting than the next?

Holy hell.

I wasn't sure if he'd meant for me to hear that particular thought or not, but at least I had my answer.

Chapter Eighteen
Hidden Heritage

The next day Amalia gave us a free day. Nox and his bandmates were rehearsing, there would be no press around, and therefore, no need for the appearance of adoring fans. The only rule was we were to stay together. The girls took a vote, and the result by popular demand was a field trip to world-famous Rodeo Drive in Beverly Hills. The other girls and I wandered in and out of shops bearing brand names I'd only seen on TV and in the movies.

Though each of us had been given a generous allowance to make some purchases, I bought nothing. Just looking at the price tag on a simple t-shirt gave me the hives. It was stunning what some people were willing to spend on clothes. If only I'd had access to this money a few months ago, when my family's land was under threat of being confiscated by the IRS.

Without Amalia's eagle eyes around, I felt comfortable stashing my phone in my purse for the outing. After about a half hour of browsing, I told my roommates I was walking down the street to sit in the sun instead of doing any more shopping.

"Okay, suit yourself. I'll let you know if we find any bargains," Kim said.

I searched for a spot out of sight of the others—a bench near the Versace store where an ornate street lamp stood adorned with two huge hanging flower baskets. Pulling my phone from my purse, I turned it on and dialed Mom. I still hadn't managed to connect with her since Grandma tipped me off to her possible status change a couple nights ago. She answered after four rings.

"Oh, Ryann honey—I'm so happy to hear from you. I miss you so much. How are you?"

"Great," I answered in a cautious tone, watching the shoppers—and fellow gawkers—take in the dazzling window displays. "California's beautiful. I'm on Rodeo Drive right now, shopping with some new friends."

"How fabulous! You're making me so jealous. I can't wait to see L.A. Davis is promising to take me soon."

"For a honeymoon?"

There was a long silence. Two women in obviously designer outfits passed by, pushing sleek baby strollers that looked like they cost about a thousand dollars each.

Finally, Mom spoke again, her voice now tinged with guilt. "Oh dear. Did someone tell you? I'm so sorry, honey. I wanted to tell you myself, but it's so hard to reach you out there with the time difference and your busy schedule. You haven't been answering your phone."

"I know. It's okay."

"Well… what do you think?"

"I'm happy for you, but I do think it's kind of fast. You haven't known him very long."

Now her voice took on a new brightness—almost too perky. "Well, that's the thing. Actually, remember I told you I worked on his campaign when I was in college? We got to know each other… quite well back then."

I sat up straight on the bench, both feet planted on the stone pavers beneath it. "What do you mean? You dated?"

"Mmmm… sort of. We couldn't actually go out—he was running for Senator. I was a sorority girl. It wouldn't have looked good."

"So then you… you slept with him. Why didn't you tell me sooner?"

"Well, it's not exactly the kind of thing you discuss with your teenage daughter. I was *planning* to tell you— when the time was right."

Sitting hard against the iron bench back, I exhaled a long breath. "Wow. You're like secret lovers reunited or something." Then a terrible thought occurred to me. "You and Daddy met in college. Did you fool around with Davis while you and Dad were together?"

"No. No, Ryann. Daddy and I had dated, but we had broken up before I got involved with Davis. Then things couldn't really progress with Davis, and I was frustrated. I told him I didn't want to see him anymore. And your daddy and I missed each other, so we got back together."

"Oh." I was overwhelmed with sadness. My mom was really going to marry this guy. He wasn't a flash in the pan or a transitional man. He really had replaced my father in her heart and now he would replace my father in our house. That was... if he intended to move in with us. Or was she planning to move in with him?

"Mom—where are you and Davis going to live when you get married?"

"He's a Georgia senator—he has to live in Georgia. So... I'll have to move there. But don't worry. We're planning to wait until you graduate for me to move. I'll travel back and forth until then. I wouldn't make you move before senior year, and I wouldn't leave you."

Ugh. She would, though. If not now, less than a year from now when I graduated high school. Things were changing so fast.

"I can't wait for you to spend some more time with him, Ryann. You are going to love him. He already loves you."

"What do you mean? He hasn't even met me."

The pause before she spoke again filled my belly with a chilling sense of nausea. "Mom?"

"He wants to *get* to know you. Davis is very eager to be a part of your life. He... wants to make up for lost time."

The chill was ice cold now. I sat in the California midday sun and felt frozen solid. "Mom... what are you talking about?"

I wasn't sure I wanted to hear the answer, but I had to. My hand holding the phone started shaking. I was terrified that I *already* knew what she was about to tell me.

"Well… I feel like we should talk about this in person. We'll talk when you get home. You and me and Davis… and Daddy."

Now my voice turned harder. "No! Tell me now—does this have something to do with why you and Daddy broke up?" A family of four turned in my direction, and I lowered my voice. "You told me you said something to Daddy you never should have said—*what was it?*"

If I'd ever possessed even a drop of the Sway, as Nox had suggested, I pulled it out right then and put it in my voice. With every note of inflection I could produce, with every ounce of persuasion I could muster, I willed my mother to tell me the truth.

"Is Davis—my *father?*"

A sob came through the phone line. I nearly threw my cell against the wall of the shop next to me but instead let it drop to the bench where it landed with a metallic clatter.

Her far-away voice called to me. "Ryann? Ryann are you still there?"

Slowly, as if in a dream, I picked up the phone and brought it back to my ear. "I'm here." My voice cracked and dry as though the hot sun had sapped the life right out of me.

Mom was weeping. "I'm so sorry, sweetheart. I was planning to tell you someday, when you were older."

"Daddy knows?"

"He does... now. When we got back together in college—well, I was pregnant. I realized it a few weeks later. Your dad never asked if the baby was his, though he had to know the truth because of the timing. He stood by me and married me. He loves you every bit as much as he would have if you were his own flesh and blood. I think he actually forgot you weren't most of the time."

She paused and sobbed again. "Until our fight over the IRS thing—I was so angry, and I said probably the most hurtful thing I could have—that maybe we'd have been better off with your 'real father.' I never should have said it. It was horrible. I hurt him so badly—that's why he... why he did what he did, and why he stayed away for so long. I was a mess for a while there—I was bitter about the way he retaliated and about what had happened with Davis, too, all those years ago. I really should have been blaming myself all this time."

I didn't respond. I couldn't. Even if I could've thought of something to say, my vocal chords wouldn't cooperate. My mom, who'd spent the past year warning me men weren't to be trusted, was the biggest liar of them all. And she was about to marry the very guy who'd left her to fend for herself when she was pregnant with his daughter—with me.

I hung up the phone and turned to the side to vomit into a conveniently placed planter. A woman nearby wrinkled her nose and turned away. Sorry Miss Rodeo Drive Shopper. Your lovely shopping day was also one of the worst of my life.

I wasn't sure how long I sat there, but I sort of came to when I heard voices calling my name from down the street. Stashing the phone back in my purse, I rose to my feet as Gigi and Bonnie ran over to me.

"Where have you been, girl? Everyone's on the bus. The driver was about to leave without you."

"We were totally freaking out. We thought maybe someone had like, kidnapped you or something."

"Are you okay," Gigi asked, her face the picture of concern. "You look kind of weird."

I nodded. "Yeah, I… I think maybe I dozed off here or something. We should get to the bus."

During the whole ride home, I re-lived the conversation again and again. The wide streets and palm trees whizzing by looked like a scene out of a TV drama—it was unreal that this was my life. I didn't even know who I was anymore.

All the givens in my world were now up for debate. My dad wasn't my dad. My mom had kept at least one huge secret from me. And I was going to have to deal with it all… alone. I was all alone. Except for Nox.

I need you. I leaned my head against the window, closing my eyes as if in prayer. *God help me, Nox—I need you right now.*

He was standing in front of the house as our bus pulled into his long driveway. The instant the hydraulic doors swished open, he rushed to the bottom of the steps, giving perfunctory greetings to the girls who got off before me. When I stepped off, he took my hand and led me inside and straight to his suite.

I didn't argue but went with him passively, feeling completely drained of energy, of thought, of any will of my own.

Closing the doors behind us, he turned me to face him, keeping his steadying hands on my shoulders. "What happened? What's going on?"

I blinked at him in confusion.

"Ryann... talk to me. Why did you say you needed me? Is everything okay?"

"You heard me," I whispered. "How..."

He nodded, his eyes searching and serious. "It's never happened to me before—hearing someone from a distance. But I've heard of it—when there's a strong connection. I thought it only happened with bonded couples, but I guess not."

The stress of the day and the weight of my new knowledge crashed over me—it was all too much to handle—I burst into tears.

Nox pulled me against his chest, wrapping his strong arms tightly around me. "Yes. Yes, I heard you. And I'm here for you. You're okay. Whatever it is, it'll be okay. Can you tell me what's going on?"

"It's not okay," I blubbered against his chest. "Everything's wrong, and it'll never be okay."

I could hear the helpless frustration in his voice. "Did you run into Emmy while you were shopping or something? Is she all right?"

I shook my head, no doubt smearing mascara across the front of his perfectly white shirt. "No. It's not Emmy. It's my mom. She's a liar. And my dad is not my dad, and... I... I'm not sure who I am anymore." A loud sob erupted from my throat and wracked my body.

Nox held me tighter. His voice was rough. "Oh baby. It's okay. I'm sorry. I'm here. Don't try to talk anymore now. You can tell me later."

He led me to the white sofa in front of the fireplace and sat down, pulling me onto his lap and guiding my head onto his shoulder. As promised, he didn't press for more information, just stroked my hair and allowed me to cry it out until I didn't have any tears left.

After a long while, I lifted my head and glanced at his face. What I saw was deep compassion and concern. Friendship for sure, and something else—something I was too emotionally drained to consider at the moment.

His eyes softened. "You ready to talk about it now?"

Inhaling deeply and heaving a heavy breath, I shook my head. "Not really. I'm so confused and tired. I should probably go back to my room." I moved to get up.

Nox's arm around my back tensed as if he was unwilling to let me go. "Don't. Stay here tonight. You can have the bed—I'll sleep on the couch."

"I don't think that's a good idea."

"And going back to your room when you've obviously been crying is? The other girls will wonder what's going on—Amalia will wonder if she sees you. How will you explain it? You're supposed to be all glamour-happy. You *can't* tell them you've been talking to your family. I know the pod girls aren't supposed to have phones."

"Oh. I didn't think of that."

"At least stay until you feel better." With a soft chuckle, he added, "We can even play Xbox if you want."

I shook my head. "No thanks. I'd rather just sit here."

Nox nodded, apparently satisfied, and lifted a remote from the side table. When he clicked a button, a fire roared to life in the fireplace. Another click and music drifted from hidden speakers at a low level, a lovely piano melody I didn't recognize.

"This is nice," I said. "Who is it?" Not that I really knew my composers.

"Oh, it's mine," he answered, sounding rather bashful.

"You play piano, too?"

"I've been re-learning. I learned as a kid—then I couldn't play in Altum—no pianos there. When I came back to California, I picked it up again. It's a great instrument for writing music."

I shook my head in wonder, beginning to relax as the beautiful melody drifted over and through me. Letting my face rest against his chest again, I stared at the beautiful fire. "Is there anything you can't do?"

"Sense people's emotions," he said. "It's a great skill to have. Imagine if I could sense the feelings of an audience,

191

and then tailor my playlist so we're always playing the perfect song to fit the mood. Every show would be epic. And I'd *still* swear you've got powerful Sway. How did a wimpy quarter-Elf get two glamours, hmm?" He squeezed his arms around me playfully. "Tell me that."

I laughed. "Well, I'm reading your emotions right now, and I'll tell you this—there's no reason to be envious. I don't even know how to use what I've got—*if* I've even *got* two glamours. They're totally wasted on me." I grinned against his chest, my mood lifting marginally.

"No." Nox kissed the top of my head. His voice was warm when he spoke again, his breath sinking into my hair. "Not wasted. They're part of all the things that make you special."

When he planted another kiss on my forehead, he let his lips linger a second, and a zing of excitement went through my belly at the heat and softness of them. For long minutes we stayed as we were, both staring at the fire, both silent. But his chest rose and fell in a faster rhythm now. Mine too.

Something was happening. Something that felt terrifying and yet sort of amazing, too.

I didn't dare look at him. I wasn't sure I wanted to see what might be there in his eyes. I wasn't sure what he'd see in mine. Finally, Nox gave me no choice. He shifted back and angled toward me so I'd have to face him.

"You *are* special, Ryann. To me. Always have been." He took a fractured breath and went on. "When you called to me today and told me you needed me, I was so afraid. I didn't know where you were, what might be happening to you. I was going crazy. Then it occurred to me to call the bus driver, and I found out you were on your way back here. I was literally pacing the driveway waiting for you." When I didn't say anything, he continued, a new vulnerability in his eyes. "I tried to tell you this before, but you wouldn't believe me…"

My heart thundered as I waited for his next words.

"I'm… in love with you." His eyes widened, like he couldn't quite believe what had come out of his own mouth, but then he swallowed hard and kept going. "When you asked me those times about my first love—it's you. You're the only one who really knows me, and I love you. I'm here for you. No matter what's going on—whatever has happened—I'm *here* for you, and I'll help you get through it. If you'll let me."

The unbelievable words, the exposed emotion in his voice, the impassioned look in his eyes yanked my heart out of the pit in my chest where it had been locked away since Lad's rejection. I had taken a risk—let myself fall in love with Lad even though I'd seen from my parents' example how badly it could turn out. And it had ended in pain. Lad was lost to me forever.

But Nox was here, offering me a second chance at love. Did I dare risk my heart again? No one else in the world felt this way about me. Certainly not Lad. And I didn't want to be alone in the world. Mom was consumed with her new relationship. Dad would move on, too, eventually. Grandma had her family in Altum, and she'd have to leave us and join them permanently when her longevity reached the point of being suspicious.

Nox stared at me with shining eyes, no doubt waiting for my reaction. Maybe for a return declaration. I wasn't ready to give him one. How could I be? I'd said those same three words to Lad only a few weeks ago.

But I did care for Nox. And he certainly seemed to care for me. He heard me when I called. He was here for me.

Very slowly, I inched toward him, lifting my chin and tilting my head in an unmistakable signal he was all-too-happy to receive. He gripped the back of my head with one hand as our mouths crashed together. He gave a pleasured groan, meeting the caresses of my tongue with his own. And then he took over, his mouth claiming mine with consuming, hungry kisses. He pulled me against him possessively, and I didn't resist. I lifted my chest against his, needing the feel of his solid body against mine.

With a lusty growling sound, Nox gripped my hips and lifted me onto his lap so I faced him, my knees straddling his hips and pressing into the soft cushion behind him. His hands dragged up to my ribcage and slid around to my back as we kissed frantically.

I didn't even have to try to read his emotions now—my response to his touch was driving Nox wild. He was fighting for control, and I was doing nothing to help things.

Lifting my hands, I held his face and kissed him back, matching his intensity stroke for stroke. My body melted into his, loving the way his skin felt under my hands, the way he made me feel small and delicate next to his vastly superior size and strength, the way he made me forget about my issues with Mom, Emmy, everything outside this room.

Sliding his hands lower, Nox pulled me tightly against his lap, and there was a moment I considered throwing all caution to the wind and letting it happen. Being close to him like this, being the recipient of his experienced touch was the best thing I'd felt in a long time.

I didn't want to think about the future, and he certainly didn't seem worried about the consequences of what we were doing. In fact, he pushed things further by breaking our kiss momentarily and stripping my tank top off in one swift move that left me slightly surprised and completely turned on.

Leaning back, he drank in the sight of me sitting astride his legs in only my bra and hiked-up skirt.

You are beautiful Ryann.

And then his lips were on my neck, and his hands were exploring all the new skin he'd uncovered. It felt incredible. But as his mouth worked its way down and his fingers moved upward, a fragment of common sense intruded.

Nox. I silently messaged him and leaned back. He only leaned forward and followed me with his mouth, not breaking delicious contact with my skin. He was *not* listening.

"Nox. We have to stop."

He lifted his head and our eyes met, his burning with unsatisfied desire, mine only barely more controlled, I'm sure.

"We *have* to," I repeated.

He closed his eyes and breathed, his fingers still clenching my sides. Finally his eyes opened. "I know. You're right." He smiled at me, wearing a look of wonder.

I smiled back, suddenly feeling shy and very exposed. Reaching for the throw blanket, Nox wrapped it around my shoulders and covered my chest.

He gave me another soft kiss. "I'm glad to see that pretty smile again. Feeling better now?"

I nodded, still amazed at what had transpired between us. "Yes."

Studying his face, I allowed myself to believe I really did have the glamour-gift of emotional IQ. I actually tried, for the first time in my life, to read another person's emotions. And they came to me with an unshakable sense of certainty. Patience. Concern. Still some barely leashed passion. And love. He really did love me. He did intend to stand beside me, no matter what came. He would do anything in his power to help me.

"Do you want to tell me what happened today?" he prompted.

To my surprise, I did. I couldn't handle all the crazy changes happening in my life all alone. In the past I would've turned to Emmy. But she wasn't here. Nox *was* here. Not only was he my friend, now I knew he loved me. I wasn't yet entirely sure how I felt about him, but as I'd admitted in that desperate silent call this afternoon, I needed him.

"I called my mom today, and she admitted she is engaged. And she also told me..." I closed my eyes and took a breath. "She told me my dad's not my biological father."

"Oh. No wonder you were upset. Did she say who is?"

I rolled my lips inward, pressing them tightly against a new round of sobs I could feel rising in my chest. "Her new fiancé—Davis."

"Wow." He blinked. "That is—that is weird. So... has she been having an affair then? During your parents' whole marriage?"

"No. She *says* no. She knew him when she was really young, in college. She was with him for a short time back then when my parents were broken up. But he was much older, and he was a senator running for re-election. He said he couldn't acknowledge her publicly, and so she broke it off with him. She and my dad got back together, but she was already pregnant with Davis's baby—with me."

Nox's body went rigid. "Did you say he's a senator? Named Davis?"

"Yeah. Davis Hart. Why do you have that look on your face?"

He did look strange. His normally tan skin had gone pale, his eyes wide and dark. He lifted a hand and cupped my face, his eyes filled with pity. "Because now I understand. Ryann... Davis Hart is—"

The double doors to Nox's suite crashed open. We both leapt to our feet, and his arms went around me in a strong protective grasp, covering my body from view.

Good thing, too. If he hadn't been holding me up, I might have dropped to the floor when a beautiful platinum-haired Elven girl strode into the room.

Followed by Lad.

CHAPTER NINETEEN
REUNION

I could hardly believe my eyes. What were they doing here? Together? My heart simultaneously exploded with joy and crashed painfully to the soles of my feet. I'd never expected to see Lad again—anywhere—least of all here in Los Angeles.

In Nox's bedroom.

"Ryann?" he gasped, probably in disbelief himself at where he'd found me.

And in what condition.

I glanced down at myself, realizing what he saw. I had on a mini-skirt... and a bra. The tank top Nox had removed minutes earlier lay a few feet away on the floor where he'd tossed it. Wiggling from Nox's hold, I grabbed the throw from where it had fallen onto the sofa and held it against my front.

Nox stepped over, picked up my shirt, and tossed it back to me as he went to stand in front of Lad and his companion—Vancia, the daughter of the Dark Elf leader and Lad's former (and once-again) fiancée.

She was completely silent and also appeared to be in shock, though her eyes were fixed on Nox instead of on me.

"What's going on?" Nox demanded of Lad. "Why are you here?"

The level of alarm in his tone surprised me—and then I got it. Only something of the greatest magnitude could have drawn Lad so far away from the center of the Light Elves kingdom, could have made him leave his people.

Lad still looked a bit stunned. I wasn't sure what he'd expected to find when he came through those doors—certainly not me sitting astride his adopted brother's lap, partially undressed.

He glanced away from Nox's face toward me, and those green eyes filled with pain. "I came looking for Ryann. Her grandmother said she would be here…" His gaze went back to Nox and turned murderous. "…with you. You were *supposed* to be keeping her safe."

Now Nox's tone hardened, and his jaw jutted out. "She is safe. And she's *happy*. If that's all you needed to know, you can go on back to the woods now. We're doing fine here, *as you can see*."

Lad's hands clenched into fists as his eyes drifted over to me again. I'd slipped the shirt back on, but I still felt utterly exposed. He'd told me to forget about him and

200

move on with my life, said I'd never see him again and there was no hope for us. He'd acted like he no longer cared.

But standing in front of me now, Lad looked like he still cared very much. In fact, he looked like his heart had been ripped out and stomped flat in front of him. Mine on the other hand was detonating in a rapid succession of blasts like the grand finale of a fireworks show.

Vancia had stayed silent, staring at Nox. When she finally spoke, her voice was choked with emotion. "We've... come with important news." Her eyes slid to me and narrowed." It concerns... the half-breed."

Oof. The term nearly knocked the breath out of me. It wasn't just the inaccuracy—I was only a quarter Elven, not half—but the disdainful tone she'd used. Clearly she knew about my history with Lad. But she had nothing to worry about. He was hers now. They were engaged. I was no longer a threat.

"What news?" Nox demanded.

Lad answered. "Ryann needs to come home. Her mother is in danger."

"What? What's going on?" I said.

"Yes," Nox agreed. "She's already been informed, and I've just learned of it myself."

My gaze bounced between the two of them, so clearly in the know, and I felt pitifully ignorant. And scared. "What? What did you learn? Why is Mom in danger?"

Vancia answered before Nox could, her eyes widening as if trying to impart some significance. "She's about to marry *my father*."

Lad finished her thought. "The leader of the Dark Elves."

Now my legs did fail me. I half-sat, half-fell onto the sofa. "Your father?" I whispered. "Dark Elves? But she's engaged to…"

And then it all made sense—the way my mom had been instantly smitten with Davis after seeing him in Atlanta. The likelihood that I possessed two different forms of inherited Elven glamour—emotional IQ and strong persuasion. I'd gotten them from *both* my parents—my mother, a half-Elf, and my father—Davis. A Dark Elf.

I wasn't a quarter Elven. I was *three* quarters Elven. More Elf than human.

More Dark than Light.

"What's the matter with her?" Vancia said, sounding aggravated. "She knows Elves exist, right? Why's she acting like she's seen a ghost?"

Lad stared at me in confusion. He wasn't aware of my parentage yet. Nox looked at me with compassion because he did know the truth.

Nox turned to Vancia—my sister. "Because your father… is *her* father."

She jerked and took a step back. "That's impossible. My father said he could not marry and sire children—that's why he adopted me when my parents died."

"Adopted?" Lad asked, looking like he wasn't quite sure where he was anymore. Apparently he didn't know *everything* about his fiancée. And apparently she *wasn't* my half-sister. I was strangely relieved—for someone who'd never actually met me, she seemed to *hate* me.

"Yes," she answered, but she wasn't looking at Lad. Her gaze returned to Nox and didn't waiver. "My parents are dead. My biological father was the Dark Elven leader, but he and my mother died in a plane crash when I was twelve along with his second-in-command. Davis was third in line to the throne. He became the Dark King and took me in and raised me."

"A plane crash..." Nox stared hard at Vancia as if seeing her for the first time. His voice was low and urgent. "Who were your parents?"

Tears filled her eyes as she answered. "They were well-known musicians, but you'd only have been a kid when they died—about twelve I think. *My best friend* and his parents died with them—or at least that's what I was *told*."

"Who *were* they?" Nox grabbed her arm, his voice ragged, his expression fierce.

Tears streamed down her face from eyes burning with recognition. "Calder and Eira."

Nox staggered backward and collapsed, sitting on the floor with his knees bent and arms across them. I got up and ran over to him, squatting beside him and touching his hot skin. He was sweating all over.

"What did you do to him?" I glared up at Vancia without taking my arms from Nox's shoulders.

Her face was blank, the skin pale and growing paler all the time. "Pappa said Gavin and Sylvie Jerrik's son died with them in the crash that killed my parents." Her gaze turned to Nox, and she stared at him as if *she* was the one seeing a ghost. Maybe in a way, she was. If their parents had worked together, had died together, she and Nox had probably met as children. In fact, it was clear they had.

Suddenly Vancia dropped beside us and threw herself across Nox's body, wrapping her arms around him and weeping. "It *is* you. I knew it."

He returned her embrace, pulling her close. "I can't believe it. I can't believe it," he said in a hoarse whisper. "I thought you were dead."

She pulled back slightly and nodded, sniffling. "That's what I believed about you. Pappa told me you were on the plane—he said you went down with them. How are you still alive?"

"My mother and I never got on the flight," he said. "And you?"

"I spent that weekend with a friend. Afterward, Pappa—Davis—came to get me and told me what had happened. He said everyone had died instantly in the crash and took me to live with him in Atlanta."

"It seems your Pappa has said a *lot* of things that aren't exactly on the up-and-up," I said, finally putting it together that Davis Hart and the leader of the Dark Elves were one and the same man—same Elf—as it turned out.

She glanced over at me as if just remembering I was there. "Are you saying he lied to me about what happened to my family then? Nox—what does your mother say about it?"

Nox spoke up now. "She's dead, too. We went into hiding after the crash. She took me to Altum—I guess it was the safest place she could think of for me. She left me there with her sister and never came back. I was raised with Lad's parents as his foster brother. How…" He shook his head, his eyes filling with wonder. "How did you find me?"

"I visited L.A. a few months ago—Pappa sent me here to have a portfolio done so I could begin modeling. I was at a nightclub and saw a poster for your band. But I didn't really believe it was you. It couldn't be you."

"Because you thought I was dead."

"Yes. And your last name was different. And you *looked* so different in the picture—I mean, kind of the same, but you're so…" Her voice trailed off in a whisper of wonder.

He nodded, understanding her unspoken words. "I know. You, too."

They looked at each other now like two children seeing Disneyworld for the first time. Lad watched them, his face unreadable. What could he be thinking now, witnessing the intimate reunion scene? Seeing his fiancée so overjoyed about another guy? Did he *know* she'd been searching for Nox?

Finally, he spoke up. His voice was soft, his expression filled with sympathy as he touched her shoulder. "Vancia, why do you think your father lied to you about Nox and his mother being on the plane?"

"Maybe…" She looked up at him wearing a stricken expression. "Maybe he believed it. He said he'd thought *I* was on the plane until later when my friend's parents called, wondering what to do with me."

"Or maybe he knew all along and he lied so you'd go with him peacefully," Nox suggested. "He's reported to have the strongest Sway of all our people. Maybe there was more to the *accident* than either of us were told."

Vancia looked like she might vomit. "I've always known he would do almost anything to get what he wanted. But this…" She shook her head, staring off into the distance before training her eyes on Nox again. "So then, you don't think our parents' deaths really were accidental. You think… you think my father is a murderer."

"No," I said, watching the room spin crazily around me. "*Your* father was a talented and beloved singer-songwriter. *My* father is the murderer."

CHAPTER TWENTY
STRONGER THAN YOU KNOW

"Ryann, are you okay?" Lad's voice was gentle in my ear as he wrapped an arm around me and led me back to the sofa.

I went with him, moving my feet across the floor on auto-pilot until we reached the seating area. There, I sank into the sofa cushions as Lad took the chair facing me.

"I think so. It's… this is a lot to take in." Reality was hitting me in quick, successive flashes of understanding. Davis had told Vancia he couldn't marry and sire children. Because he'd *already* bonded with someone—my mother. And he'd already fathered a child. Me.

If Vancia didn't hate me before, she would now. First, I'd interfered in her long-arranged royal wedding, and now I had stolen her father. Did she also blame me for monopolizing her long lost childhood friend?

I glanced over at Nox, still sitting on the floor. She was on her knees in front of him, gripping his hands and talking to him in low tones. How bizarre. I'd just learned my father was a Dark Elf. They'd just learned of each other's survival after all these years. The shock filling the room was almost visible, like fog or an indoor storm cloud.

Vancia listened intently to whatever Nox was telling her. Then he lifted his head, searching the room. Our eyes connected, and his sparked with warmth.

Are you all right? He asked silently.

I'm okay. You?

He shrugged and nodded. *A little blown away, but yeah. I'm good.*

I gave him a small smile, and then my eyes drifted to Vancia's face. She was not smiling. She was studying Nox.

And then she looked my way, shooting me a brief but furious glare. What was that about? A warning? I wasn't even touching her fiancé while she was practically glued to my guy. Maybe the idea of a "half-breed" with *any* Elven guy offended her? Maybe she didn't like the fact that I could communicate in the Elven way? She probably didn't think I was worthy of her language *or* her friend.

"Ryann... Ryann," Lad attempted to recapture my attention. "I need you to focus. We've got to get back to Mississippi immediately," he said. "This is much worse than I thought. Your mother needs your help. And I believe it's obvious now who killed my father as well."

That snapped me back to the moment. "Oh my gosh—you're probably right. But I can't leave Emmy here. I have to bring her home with me."

"There's no time. The sooner we get your mom away from Davis the better."

"But we're going to see Emmy tomorrow. Nox is taking us to training camp—she'll be there. I'm so close now—I have to try."

"How?" Lad asked.

"Nox is going to trade me for her—to Reggie Dillon— he's the Dark Elf who has her now. And then I'll escape."

Lad's face contorted into a horrified scowl as he came to his feet, fist clenched. "No—that's too dangerous—I won't allow it," he yelled.

His word choice and kingly tone irked me. It reminded me of the high-handed way he'd treated me the day he told me to go away and never contact him again. And I wasn't his concern any longer—he had a *fiancée* to worry about now. Before I'd even realized what I was doing, I was off the couch, too, bowing up to him, pointing a finger at his chest.

"You might be king of the woods back at Altum, but you are not *my* king—you don't give me orders. I'm surprised you're even here—you don't care about me." He flinched as I continued my rant. "I *am* going to get Emmy and bring her home, and you can't stop me."

He backed off a bit and lowered his voice. "How Ryann? You can't possibly pull this off."

"Maybe she can." Sometime during our argument, Nox had made his way over to us with Vancia following close behind. He stood beside me and slid an arm around my back. "In fact, Ryann may be the perfect person to do it. She's like a secret weapon. She looks and acts human—as far as anyone here knows she *is* human. But she's three-quarters Elven. She's not susceptible to most glamour. I've seen her display Elven abilities—the Sway, for example. She's stronger than you know, Lad."

Lad wheeled around and snarled in Nox's face. "I *know* her—*far* better than you do. And obviously, I'm more concerned about her safety than you are. How could you even *think* of letting her risk herself by going into a fan pod, especially one run by a much older, stronger Elf than any of us?"

Now it was my turn to raise my voice. "No one is *letting* me—or *not* letting me—do anything. I'm making my own decisions. And I've decided this is the best way—the only way—to get Emmy back. There's no point in wasting time arguing over it. Either get with the program, Lad, or... get out of the way. I know you have *more important* things and more important *people* to worry about. Why don't you go back home and take care of *them*?"

Now his face was the portrait of anguish. His shoulders sagged, and his voice pleaded with me. "Ryann... please don't do this. You don't understand..."

"No. I do. I'm on my own. You said it yourself. You refused to help me, and so I found my own way. And it's working just fine so far. I don't need you." I shifted my eyes to his beautiful female companion in a pointed look. "And you clearly don't need me."

My voice broke as I spoke the last few words. How humiliating. Suddenly, I just wanted him gone. I couldn't take any more of this. Lifting my chin, I reached over and groped for Nox's hand. He clasped my fingers in a reassuring squeeze.

Directing his words at Lad, he said, "Well, Ryann and I have lots of planning to do. I'll walk you out."

Lad looked like he might protest, but he said nothing. Together, Nox and I walked to the doors of the suite and opened them, waiting for Lad and Vancia to exit the room. Lad got the message. He walked out the door without a glance at me or Nox. But as Vancia passed us, she and Nox locked eyes for a moment.

Had the old friends shared an unspoken message? If so, what was it?

Not my business, that's what.

"Thank you," I whispered to Nox as we fell into step behind our guests, following them to the front doors of his mansion.

He said nothing but gripped my hand tighter and gave me a sweet smile.

Stepping outside, both Vancia and Lad turned around to face us. "Well, goodbye for now," she said to Nox.

"What will you do about your father?" he asked.

She crossed her arms and shook her head, looking off to the side. "I'm not sure. I don't know what to think right now. I need more information. We were estranged after the cancelled wedding." She flicked a glance at me. "But I'm back in his good graces. Let me see what I can find out when I get back home."

Did she mean Altum—or Atlanta, where Davis lived? And why did she think Davis would tell her anything? I watched her go down the steps of Nox's mansion and walk to the limo parked in the drive. I didn't trust her. She *acted* like she was suspicious of Davis, but by her own admission, she was in his good graces. For all I knew, she was lying to Nox about what she knew about the accident—about him.

She could be tricking Lad as well. The plane crash was five years ago. She'd lived with Davis ever since, called him "Pappa." She could easily be working with him against the Light Elves. She was, after all, a Dark Elf.

Lad hadn't followed her to the car. He stood facing me, still wearing a look of deep concern and seemingly reluctant to leave.

"Ryann... please reconsider. I have to leave tomorrow. If I had more time, I might be able to—"

The ache in his voice touched my heart. Which made me mad. My heart and Lad had no more business together. He'd made his choice, and his choice wasn't me.

"There *is* no more time—you said it yourself," I bit out. "Thank you for bringing the warning about my mom and Davis. I'll call her. I'm guessing she won't listen to me, though because I think she's pretty deep under his glamour. And I'll talk to Grandma and let her know what's happening—oh my God." I had to gasp for air as it hit me. "He's probably glamoured her, too." This was a mess, and I had to fix it. "Just don't worry about it. I'll be home very soon. *With* Emmy."

Nox rested a large hand on Lad's shoulder. "She'll be fine, brother. I'll make sure of it."

Leveling him with a deadly glare, Lad shrugged off Nox's hand, spun around, and strode quickly toward Vancia, who waited by the limo, still gazing back at Nox.

When they'd driven away, I let out a long breath. "Okay. So… we have a lot to talk about."

"Understatement of the century," he said, and we went inside together, hand in hand.

Chapter Twenty-One
TRADE

My podmates and I filed off the bus at the Los Angeles Tremors practice facility in Orange County the next day, dressed in the short shorts and team t-shirts provided for us by Amalia. I wasn't sure how much advance notice she'd been given in order to arrange things like wardrobe for the pod, but she hadn't seemed the least bit surprised or stressed by the spontaneous plan. Maybe this was how it always worked in the celebrity fan pod world.

Cameras rolled and clicked as we passed the media area near the observation deck. No doubt viewers of sportscasts around the globe would be treated to visions of adoring young female fans worshipping at the altar of Reggie Dillon, and his already enormous fame would grow even bigger. Nox was not just offering Reggie a fresh "shopping experience" by bringing his fan pod here, he was also lending him some of his star power and spotlight. A win-

win for everyone—except for the fan pod members themselves.

We spread out and found seats in the fan zone while my eyes searched the sea of similarly dressed girls for Emmy. Unless she'd gotten sick or stayed back at Reggie's mansion for some other reason, she would be here. I'd finally have my chance to talk to her and hopefully talk some sense into her.

As casually as I could, I made my way toward Reggie's fan pod girls, always keeping my eyes on the practice field and cheering and clapping at appropriate moments so as not to seem suspicious. Finally reaching the invisible boundary between our group and his, I scanned the spectators again. My heart leapt—there she was!

Emmy was standing with a tight group of four girls—a cute Asian girl, two blondes, and another girl with creamy brown skin similar to Shay's.

It took everything in me not to drop my façade and run to her and grab her up in a hug. But that wouldn't be very fan-podish of me. I wasn't even sure if someone under glamour would be able to recognize someone from home—my suitemates certainly didn't seem to think of the families and friends they'd left behind.

Squeezing past a few bodies at a time, I worked my way toward her. And then there we were, face to face for the first time in weeks. Well, I was face-to-face with her—her eyes were on the field, tracking Reggie Dillon's every move.

I reached out and touched her forearm. "Emmy?"

Her stare broke. She glanced at me, a strange look passing over her face. Trying to tap into whatever Elven glamour I might possess and read her feelings, I got a distinct impression of confusion, even fear.

"Emmy," I repeated. "It's me, Ryann." It was bizarre to introduce myself to my best friend since preschool, but there was no recognition in Emmy's eyes. My heart sank. I had hoped my voice might jar her from the fog she was in.

"Ryann?" She shook her head, her expression blank.

"From home. From Deep River." *It's not working.* I had to do something to jar her memory. How would I ever convince Emmy to slip away with me if she didn't even know who I was?

I've seen how the other girls in the house react when you make a suggestion.

Nox's recent words came back to me. He was convinced I had powerful Sway in my bloodline, and now that I knew who my real father was, maybe he was right.

Davis was chairman of the powerful Senate Science and Technology committee—he was obviously incredibly influential. He'd even been able to glamour my mom, who was half-Elven and apparently Grandma Neena, too—he must have—she'd met him and never mentioned he was Elven.

So it was likely powerful persuasion was his main glamour ability. In fact, considering all the elections he'd won and the lofty position he held in the National government, he was one of the foremost practitioners of the Sway, as Nox had said.

Focusing my mind, I touched Emmy's arm again and got her attention. When she was looking directly at my eyes, I put my strongest intention behind my words and said, "Come with me."

She immediately took a step away from her "friends" and toward me.

"Hey, Emmy. Where're you going?" one of the blondes asked.

"We're going to the bathroom. Be right back," I called back over my shoulder, already leading Emmy away from the field and toward the back of the crowd.

"Where are we going?" Emmy stumbled along beside me, but I still wasn't sure if she had any idea who I was. For all I knew, she was merely following "orders" and was still a glamourized automaton—only this time under my glamour instead of Reggie's.

We'd nearly made it to the parking lot when a harsh voice snapped my head around.

"Girls! Ryann—what do you think you're doing?"

Ugh. It was Amalia. Did the woman have eyes in the back of her head and on each side as well? Maybe that was her glamour—extreme observation skills. Time to pretend brainwashed innocence.

"Um, looking for the bathroom? Someone said there are porta-potties around here somewhere."

Her expression was pure disgust. "They're over there." She pointed the opposite direction of where we were headed. "And who is this? She's not one of ours."

Dread sliced through my midsection. I couldn't tip her to what I was up to. "Um... I don't know her name. She said she knew where the bathroom was? I guess she was mixed up, though?"

It took Amalia a few long strides to reach us. "I'll lead you there, so you don't get *lost*." Her eyes narrowed as she studied me like a particularly fascinating species of insect. "And you—she nodded to Emmy. Get back with your pod. Ask your house manager for permission before leaving your group."

Emmy immediately turned and walked away, without another glance at me. A sinking sensation pulled at me. *So close. So freaking close.*

Amalia wrapped her skinny fingers around my upper arm and basically marched me toward the porta potties. Though everything in me wanted to shrug out of her grasp, I had to force myself to allow her touch.

After staying in the porta potty for a reasonable amount of time to support my cover story, I opened the door. Amalia was waiting for me. Docilely I allowed her to lead me back to my pod and then waited out the remainder of the seemingly never-ending practice session, trying futilely to make eye contact with Emmy again from across the observation area. She never even looked my way.

So, a trade it was.

We might have been able to avoid it, if I'd been successful at slipping away with Emmy, but now there was no other way. Nox had to trade me for her. I'd get out of Reggie's estate on my own later.

At the end of practice, Reggie came to the sidelines where Nox had been standing and watching for the past half hour. The two of them shook hands then did some manly back-slapping, laughing, and smiling. Clearly Nox was one of the Elven bad boys club as far as he was concerned.

Only I knew better. Or I hoped I did. If not, I was about to find myself at the mercy of one of the hugest and most intimidating men I'd ever seen.

I'd only glimpsed Reggie Dillon in passing on TV, back when my dad was at home and watching football on Sundays. I'd never paid close attention, and since Daddy had moved out, I hadn't watched any games at all. But now—up close and in person—it was clear to me Reggie was indeed Elven.

He was exceptionally tall, even for an Elf, his height exceeding Nox's by several inches. And though he'd been playing a rough sport for many years, his face held the improbable handsomeness all Elven males possessed. His smile was white and dazzling against his dark skin, and his eyes sparkled as he conversed with Nox. About what? All the fresh delicacies his new Elven buddy had brought along for him to sample?

I couldn't stop the churning sensation that thought produced in my gut, but I also knew it was a good thing. We *needed* Reggie to be interested in Nox's stable of girls. In *me*, particularly. We needed him to be willing to make a trade. I could only hope he'd find me appealing enough to hand Emmy over in exchange.

After a few minutes, both Reggie and Nox turned their attention toward the observation deck—toward us. Reggie's eyes scanned our group, but Nox's made immediate contact with mine. He leaned his head toward Reggie and pointed in my direction. My heart slammed against my sternum. This was it. Would Reggie turn his nose up at me? Or would he agree with Nox's recommendation?

I saw the moment his decision was made. The football player's face split into another dazzling grin, and he nodded and offered Nox a huge hand for high-fiving. I pretended not to notice, casually turning to a girl next to me to ask her if she knew what time it was. Of course she didn't. None of us were allowed to carry phones, but probably all of us were used to having them because very few wore watches.

Someone tapped me on the shoulder, and I turned to see a Tremors trainer. "How'd you like to meet the quarterback?" the man asked.

He didn't appear to be Elven—he was stocky and rather short—but then, he didn't have to be. The whole team wasn't made of Elves. They'd be unbeatable if they were.

I put on an expression I hoped conveyed delighted surprise and followed the trainer down to the sideline area and over to where Nox and Reggie stood.

"What's your name?" Nox asked me.

"Ryann," I answered quickly, understanding he was pretending for Reggie's sake.

"Well, Ryann, this is Reggie Dillon. Reggie, meet Ryann."

"Ryann," Reggie purred in the voice of a man used to having women fall at his feet. "So glad you could make it to training camp today. Did you enjoy watching?"

I gave him an adoring smile. "I did. Especially watching *you*."

He beamed back at me in return then cast a conspiratorial look over at Nox, who was definitely *not* beaming. "This one's going to be fun."

I fought the urge to stomp his big toe. He assumed I was halfway to being glamoured by him already. And apparently he was going to agree to the trade. If so, I'd have to make my escape quickly, based on the look in his eye. I fervently hoped he'd had a rough day on the field and was *really* tired tonight.

When I darted a glance at Nox's face, the displeasure there was loud and clear.

Be cool, I warned him silently. He gave a terse nod.

Replacing the frown with a lascivious grin and directing his gaze at Reggie's fan pod, he drawled. "All right then. Where's mine?"

"You can have pretty much whichever one you want," Reggie said. "I've tried almost all of them already."

"Excellent." Making a speculative *hmmm* sound in his throat, Nox pointed out Emmy as if his finger had just happened to land where it had in the crowd. "I'll take that one."

"Oh man, I'm sorry. I said you could have *pretty much* any one. Not that one, though. I'm not done with her yet. Wicked Southern accent—drives me crazy—and Vallon recommended her especially to me."

Now Nox did dart his eyes at me. I widened mine at him. *What are we going to do?*

I'm not sure. Let me think, he replied.

"Now you have me intrigued." Nox chuckled. "What about for just a night?"

Reggie tipped his head back, laughing loudly. "We always want the ones we can't have, don't we my friend? Have patience. You'll have her—and anyone else you want—eventually. Why not take that one tonight?" He waved toward a tiny redhead who looked like she could easily be a ninth-grader. God I hoped she wasn't. "She's *very* enthusiastic," he added with a wink.

Nox shot me another glance, and he didn't even have to tell me—I knew he was beginning to balk at the prospect of sending me off with Reggie and *without* even procuring Emmy in exchange.

Don't worry. I assured him. *This will give me more time with her—I can work on her, get her to remember who she is and why she needs to go home. We'll escape together.*

Hopefully, my mental tone came across more confident than I felt. I had no idea how effective my glamour would actually be on Emmy, and no doubt arranging an escape for two would be even more challenging than an escape for one. I wasn't exactly Jason Bourne. My resistance to glamour was the only thing I had going for me.

"Fine," Nox ground out, sounding surly and dissatisfied.

His tone earned another laugh from Reggie. "I'll make it up to you next time, my friend. You can take anyone you want and give me the one you want to unload." Slapping Nox on the back, he departed, heading for the field house where the rest of his teammates had already gone.

Before Nox and I could exchange any words, a tall black-haired beauty approached us from the side and grabbed my elbow. "Come with me."

I assumed she was Reggie's house manager, and he'd sent her the message to collect me. Her other hand was wrapped around the wrist of the little redhead. "And this one—Megan—is yours."

She unceremoniously pushed the girl toward Nox, who looked from her to me. Now his eyes held a spark of panic. He'd finally realized I was leaving him—right here, right now.

"Wait—" he started to protest.

"Is there a problem?" the dark-haired house manager asked. "Was this not the one you wanted?"

It's fine, Nox. I'll be fine. I'll be home as soon as possible. With Emmy. Home, meaning his house in Malibu.

With one last helpless glance at me, Nox barked, "No, it's fine. She'll do."

She gave him a knowing grin. "First trade, huh? You've got to watch out for Reggie. He's an expert. He'll rob you blind."

With a wink for Nox and barely a glance for me, the woman tightened her fingers on my arm and led me away toward a waiting bus. Reggie's pod members were already boarding. As I put my foot on the first step of the boarding ramp, I risked one last glance back at Nox.

He stood in the same place I'd left him, hands hanging loose by his sides, wearing a forlorn expression. *Be careful,* he messaged me. *I will have you back with me soon—one way or the other. And stay OUT of his suite.*

The last part was practically a shout in my brain. He didn't have to tell me twice. The less time I spent alone with Reggie Dillon, the better as far as I was concerned.

Chapter Twenty-Two
Reggie's House

It would have been ideal if I could've managed to sit with Emmy on the bus—maybe I'd have been able to glamour her sufficiently during the ride so we could disembark and walk right off the estate together when we got there.

But my luck was not that good. I was one of the last girls to board thanks to the wheeling and dealing I'd been a part of. Emmy already had a seatmate, like all the other girls. The only space available was next to the house manager. Great. There would be no influencing *anyone* on this ride.

"So, Ryann—that's your name, right? I'm Ingrid. I'm the house manager for Reggie's fan pod. You'll be taking Megan's bed in her old suite tonight." Under her breath she added as she turned toward the window, "That's *if* you get to *go* to bed tonight."

I nodded and kept my face carefully blank, but her words had lit a panic fire inside me. Probably no one knew Reggie's tendencies better than this woman—it was her job to make sure all his whims and desires were met—and she seemed to think he'd be summoning me to his suite *tonight*.

I closed my eyes and concentrated on Emmy—on why I was doing this. Then to calm my nerves, I pictured my log house back in Mississippi. I saw the faces of Grandma, Mom, and Dad—all the people who cared about me, who were worried about me and needed me to come home. A vision of Lad came unbidden to my mind, probably spurred by his visit last night.

Clearly, he no longer belonged in that group, but apparently the message *still* hadn't gotten through to my heart.

"Are you all right?" Ingrid's sharp voice startled my eyelids open.

I met her gaze. "Yes. I sometimes have a problem with motion sickness." And then a brilliant idea occurred to me—something that might keep me out of Reggie's suite tonight. "At *least* I think that's what it is. My family had the flu when I left a few days ago. I hope I don't have it."

"The flu?" Ingrid looked annoyed, but I knew she wasn't worried for herself. Elves didn't get human illnesses like flu. "I certainly hope not—I don't want you infecting the other girls. Maybe I should have you quarantined for a few days."

Dang it. That wouldn't work either. I couldn't be kept away from Emmy for a few days. I needed to get to her immediately and make quick work of this then get home to help convince Mom that Davis wasn't the dream guy she believed him to be.

"I'm sure I don't. Actually, I think I'm feeling a bit better already. I've always had carsickness, since I was a kid."

She sat back in her seat, looking somewhat relieved but studying my face. "Good. Well, be sure to tell me if you feel worse again. We have a full schedule. The last thing we need is a houseful of sick girls."

Okay, so playing sick wasn't going to keep me from Reggie's clutches. Maybe I could talk to Emmy this afternoon and convince her to escape with me before Reggie's *appetites* awakened.

Reggie's mansion was in the Hollywood Hills off Nichols Canyon Road. The multi-level concrete, steel, and glass structure was in a gated compound, built into the side of a hill with panoramic views of the canyons below.

Ingrid herded us through the house, past an incredible marble kitchen and a sleek, modern entertaining space toward a separate wing. When we got there and I saw how spread out the fan pod quarters were, I worried. Would I even see Emmy? What if her room was on the opposite end of our wing? It would be awfully suspicious of me to seek her out. I wanted to do this casually, as if we'd just run into each other and started chatting.

I fought to keep Emmy in my line of sight so I'd know where her room was. I'd have to find an excuse to go there—maybe pretend to be confused and wander into her room by "mistake," thinking it was mine.

And then a miracle happened. Or a very lucky coincidence. Whatever it was, I felt like leaping up and tapping the ceiling when I saw the back of Emmy's head go into a room and followed as Ingrid led me into the same room right after her. Were Megan and Emmy suitemates?

I couldn't let my excitement show. I wasn't supposed to know Emmy, and I was supposed to be glamoured, so I shouldn't have any vested interest in which room I would sleep in. I kept my emotions in check and forced myself to pay attention as Ingrid gave me the house rules and showed me to my new bed.

Megan's things were still scattered about—a hairbrush and makeup bag on the bed, socks hanging out of one drawer of her dresser. Her hot pink suitcase peeked out from under the bedspread. It looked like she'd rushed to get ready on time this morning, and naturally, she'd assumed she'd be coming back here. I guessed she was having a similar experience at Nox's house, taking over my room, checking out my abandoned belongings, meeting Gigi and my other former suitemates.

"Don't worry about your things—they'll be sent over shortly," Ingrid said, anticipating my question. "And we'll send Megan's things to her. This sort of thing happens all the time. You'll feel right at home here soon. You have two hours before dinner to get to know your roommates." She spun and left the room.

"Hey, you look familiar. You're the girl who was looking for the porta-potty. Ryann, right?" Emmy said with a friendly smile.

My heart broke at her disassociated tone. "Yeah. You're Emmy, right?"

She nodded and introduced me to her other suitemates, a girl from Boston named Kerri and a girl from Florida named Tara. They all fell into a discussion of Megan and what it might be like to be forced to leave Reggie's exalted presence and go to another fan pod.

"What's Nox Knight like?" Kerri asked.

Tara wrinkled her nose. "I'm not a big fan of rockers— they're usually assholes. Athletes are much nicer."

"And hotter," Kerri agreed.

All three looked at me, waiting on my assessment of my former pod master.

"Um, well, Nox is nice. Not an asshole at all, actually, he's—"

"Well, obviously *you're* going to say that." Kerri laughed. "You *love* him. Like we love Reggie. I'd die if I got sent away."

I wanted to argue that I *didn't* love Nox but quickly thought better of it. It would be stupid to reveal my objectivity, something none of these girls possessed. Reggie's glamour Kool-Aid was obviously every bit as strong as Nox's. The girls here were just as helplessly enslaved.

But *how* was it happening, exactly? I still didn't understand it. As my new suitemates filled me in on the glories of Reggie, I let the question turn over in my mind. How much time could he possibly be spending with them? And how long did the glamour last outside his presence?

From what I'd seen at Nox's house, he spent hardly any time with his fan pod members at all—yet they stayed focused on him to an obsessive degree, staring at his pictures on social media and The Hidden's website, watching his videos on You Tube, listening to his music, and generally gorging themselves on all things Nox.

It looked to be the same story here. As I glanced around the room, I saw a TV in the corner, its volume down low, broadcasting an interview with Reggie. A female network sports reporter, Elven from the looks of her, was holding a mic to his handsome face, and Reggie smiled charmingly while discussing the team's readiness for the upcoming season.

Emmy's laptop stood open on her bed, and video of a Tremors game played on the screen. I knew the team wasn't playing right now, so it had to be a recorded game.

Emmy had always been into jocks, but this was extreme, even for her. She loved SEC sports, but I'd never known her to be an NFL fan and certainly not a Tremors fan. Now she was watching their game *re-broadcasts*? I couldn't imagine anything more boring.

Posters of Reggie playing, Reggie sweating, Reggie smiling and posing in a midriff-baring jersey and tight football pants decorated the walls of our room. On the ceiling above the bed where I'd sleep tonight (hopefully, please God, let me sleep tonight) was a poster of him in a locker room setting, holding a football and wearing only a towel and a smile.

Um yeah. I did *not* like the idea of lying under his predatory gaze, either in a photo or in person. I needed to get this job done fast.

After a little more conversation, Kerri and Tara went back to their room on the other side of our shared and adjoining bathroom, finally leaving me and Emmy alone. I shut the bathroom door and joined Emmy on her bed where she'd settled in to watch the outdated game. This was my chance to get through to her.

"Emmy?"

"Hmm?" She gave me a brief, glazed-looking glance then returned her eyes to the computer screen.

"Emmy, can we talk?"

"Talk?" she repeated, looking no more tuned-in and interested than before.

Frustrated, I reached over and closed the laptop. She gave me an offended glare. "Hey! I was watching that."

"Sorry. I need to talk to you."

"About what? Reggie?"

"Not exactly. Well, sort of. Emmy—do you not remember me at all?" Now I made a conscious effort to turn on my glamour. I focused all my intent on influencing her to listen and believe me. "We are friends. We've been friends since we were four. And I came here to save you."

"Save me? From what?"

"You're in danger. You're not yourself. Look at where you are, Emmy. You're not even with Vallon anymore—that was what you wanted more than anything, remember? You've loved his movies your whole life. You worshipped the ground he walked on. And now you're in someone else's fan pod—someone you've never even mentioned to me. Doesn't that strike you as strange? And you don't even seem upset about it."

She shook her head, her eyebrows pulling together and her mouth turning down in a bewildered frown. "I'm... not upset."

"Because you're not thinking for yourself. Someone is controlling your mind—controlling *you*—and putting you into positions you didn't choose, maybe making you do things you don't want to do."

Now her chin bobbed up and down, the frown deepening. "I didn't want to go to Reggie's room. I didn't want to do those... I wanted to be with Vallon." Her eyes glistened with newly formed tears. I could read fear from her again, as well as the ever-present confusion.

"That's why I'm here. I'm going to get you out of here. We're leaving—tonight."

Emmy stared intently into my eyes, and I saw a spark of recognition, a glimmer of my old friend. "Ryann?"

I laughed, unable to contain my joy. "Yes. It's me. I'm here—I came here to get you."

Tears spilled over her eyelids and she did a little laugh-cry thing as she threw her arms around me. "Ryann. I want to go home."

She sobbed again, and I nodded against her shoulder, squeezing her tightly. "Yes. Yes, we're going home."

Drawing back to look at my face, she asked, "When?" Her voice was full of hope.

"Right now. Let's go. Do you need to bring anything with you?"

She shook her head and rose from the bed to follow me to the door. "What are we gonna do, Ryann? I don't have any money to fly home. Do you?"

"Don't worry about that. N—" I stopped myself from saying Nox's name. I didn't want there to be any chance of his being implicated in our escape. "Someone will help us. I'll call him when we get away from the estate, and he'll come pick us up."

And I knew he would. In my heart, I had no doubt Nox would help us, help me. That he'd do anything I needed. Holding Emmy's hand, I opened the door to our room and pulled her out into the hallway. It was crowded with girls in bikinis.

Kerri turned to us. "What are you doing? You can't go out to the pool like that. Go get your suits on."

"Oh, I uh…"

"Didn't you hear the announcement? Reggie's invited us to swim with him. And there are some other super-hot celebs out there. It's a pool party!" Tara squealed and bounced, testing the limits of her tiny triangle top.

Dang. Ingrid had said we had two hours free. When had this come up?

I didn't have to consider it long before realizing we were all responding to Reggie's whim. He was probably hot after returning from practice and decided there was no better way to cool off than in his Olympic-sized pool surrounded by half-naked adoring women. I should have been thrilled he wanted us only *half*-naked. These girls would no doubt take it all off for him if he suggested it.

But there was still a way out of this. In fact, this new development could be a good thing. If I could stall a bit, Emmy and I would be able to sneak through the house and out the front entrance while everyone else was splashing around out back.

"I don't have my suit with me," I said, feigning disappointment.

Emmy came to life beside me. "I've got an extra—in my room—you can borrow it."

She grinned at me, and I gave her an approving nod. Truthfully, I wanted to hug her. This was perfect—the exact opportunity we needed for escape. We'd go back to the room, wait until the others were outside, then make a break for it.

"Great. Listen y'all—we're gonna go back and find a suit for me, I'll get changed, and we'll meet you out there."

And then someone tapped me on the back. I spun around to see Ingrid giving me the coldest smile I'd ever beheld.

"There will be no need for *borrowed* swimwear. I have this for you. It's brand-new. It's Versace."

I had to swallow my heart before answering. First, because it scared me to death that she'd been standing right behind me as I tried to concoct a scheme to escape. And second, because what dangled from her fingertip resembled a hair ribbon more than an actual garment.

"Oh. Wow. That's… great. So generous."

"It's not generosity," she snapped. "It's what Reggie wants. He likes his girls to look good. Now get in there and put it on." She dropped the ribbon into my palm. "Emmy—grab your suit and go with the others. You can change in the pool house. I'll make sure your new roommate finds her way to the pool deck."

Emmy snapped into action, obeying Ingrid's orders and emerging from the room in under a minute with a yellow bikini in hand. Giving me a last searching glance over her shoulder, she followed the other girls down the hall.

"You two seem to be getting along well," Ingrid said in a measured tone.

I made sure my answering tone was all small-town-girl innocence. "Yes. She's nice. And I like my room. Okay… I'll go get changed."

Five minutes later I stood in front of the full-length closet door mirror, almost in tears. I couldn't go out there—anywhere—in this swimsuit. Donatella Versace was known for her daring, body-baring designs, and she'd outdone herself on this one. Not only was I being asked to shed all my street clothes, I'd have to drop every scrap of modesty I possessed to wear this in public.

The suit would officially have been called a one-piece, but when I walked out of this room, parts of me that had never seen the sun would be exposed for the world to see. It was black, with a halter-style top that plunged to my lower ribcage. The halter straps themselves barely covered the centers of my breasts, revealing side cleavage on *both* sides. The top and bottom halves of the suit were joined by a metallic gold ring over my belly button.

Matching gold rings at each hip anchored the bottom half of the suit, which was no more generous than the top. It consisted of a tiny panel of black fabric that barely covered my bikini zone in the front and a mortifying never-in-my-life G-string in the back.

Cringing, I turned around and peeked over my shoulder at the rear view.

Oh dear God. It was worse than I'd expected. I looked basically nude from behind. My eyes went to the window. Was it wired with a house alarm? Maybe I could climb out and hitch a ride back to Nox's? No. Emmy was here. I couldn't leave her.

I turned back around to the mirror, my face a twisted image of anxiety and my hands wringing each other white from loss of circulation.

A knock sounded at the door, making me jump.

"Are you dressed? What's taking so long?"

I called a shaky answer back to Ingrid, my guard dog. "Almost. Just a minute."

Oh God. I had to do it. If I refused to wear the Emperor's-new-swimwear, Ingrid would know I wasn't glamoured.

And then Reggie would know.

And then the word would no doubt travel up the Elven chain of command—to the council? To the leader of the Dark Elves himself—Davis? That would put not only me in danger, but Emmy, and Mom, and even Nox, who should have "known better" that I wasn't actually under his glamour.

Chapter Twenty-Three
Pool Party

I swallowed the enormous lump in my throat and wiped my expression clean of worry and doubt, doing my best to replace it. Joyful anticipation was too much to ask of myself, so I went for untroubled serenity.

I walked to the door and opened it, stepping out into the hallway with a confident stride. I shivered in the air conditioning as Ingrid checked me over like she was inspecting a package of meat at the grocery store.

"Good. That's perfect on you. You have a good build for a—come on—let's join the others."

Ugh. The others. I wasn't worried about the other girls—they were in the same boat as I was, probably uncomfortable in their own assigned swimwear. It was Reggie who concerned me. My goal had been to fly under his radar. But wearing this suit, I might as well have a black box strapped to my butt. One look and his radar would probably be pinging off the charts.

Maybe he was already fully involved with the other girls and drinking copious amounts of adult beverages. I would slip into the water and hide before he spotted me.

That hope was dashed the instant I stepped onto the pool deck. Reggie was not in the water, not involved with any girls. Yes *they* were in the water, splashing and laughing and screaming in that *please look at me* way girls do when there are guys around and they want to be sure they're noticed.

And they *were* capturing the guys' attention. Reggie stood near the outdoor bar, surrounded by a group of men—some clearly fellow athletes, others might have been actors—it was hard to tell. They were all so unnaturally good-looking and camera-ready any one of them would look right at home on the set of a men's fashion magazine photo shoot.

Their eyes were on the pool where two sets of girls were having a sort of wrestling match in the shallow end, each team comprised of a girl riding another's shoulders. Reggie raised his hands, clapping them over his head at their antics.

I followed Ingrid, and as we neared the group, averted my eyes from the men. Walking by in this swimsuit and making eye contact would probably equal some sort of invitation in their eyes.

But before looking away, I caught a glimpse of a tall, dark-haired man from the back. His shoulders were wide, his waist narrow, his legs long and strong. The way he stood reminded me of… *my God. Nox is here.*

Perhaps noticing the other guys noticing *me*, he turned around. Our eyes locked. And then his gaze dropped. And stayed. Right on my chest and all that exposed side cleavage. Then it moved to my waist, my belly button, my hips, down my legs and slowly back up.

His jaw literally dropped open. I'd never seen that particular expression before on any guy in my entire life. It was a look of shock coupled with raging desire.

My eyes widened involuntarily at his expression, and then I tore my gaze away and locked it on the back of Ingrid's head. As we passed directly in front of the group, I could tell they were no longer watching the shallow end wrestling match. Another spectacle had commandeered their interest. The non-existent back of my barely-there suit.

There were appreciative noises, lewd comments, and suggestions of future trades. *Awesome.* I'd just become the prize Holstein at the cattle auction. Instead of flying under the radar, I was up on the block for bids.

I didn't let on that I'd heard their remarks or that I cared about the eyes boring into my backside. Ingrid left me with the other girls at the deep end of the pool, and I dived under the surface, instantly relieved to be away from the hungry gazes above.

Coming up for air, I glanced around, searching for Emmy. She was hanging on the side of the pool with some other girls, facing a huge outdoor TV screen. Naturally, it was playing highlights of Reggie's team interspersed with interview clips.

When a girl in a red G-string bikini got out of the water near the men and sashayed toward the diving board, I swam over to Emmy.

"Hi y'all," I said to the group. No answer. Nothing. Everyone, including Emmy, kept staring at the screen.

I tapped Emmy on the shoulder. "Hey, you want to swim over there with me? We can finish our earlier conversation," I said meaningfully.

She turned to me and blinked as if the sun were in her eyes. "What conversation? Were we talking about Reggie?"

"No. The *other* conversation." I lowered my voice to a whisper. "You know—the one about our *plans*." I gave her the wide eyes and raised eyebrows.

She shook her head. "What plans?"

Oh no. What had happened between our bedroom door and this pool? We'd discussed an escape not twenty minutes earlier. Now Emmy didn't seem to have any idea what I was talking about, and the disconnected look was back in her eyes. She turned back to the big screen.

And then it hit me. *That's* what had happened. The screen. The video. Something about the video of Reggie had mesmerized her to the point that my earlier efforts seemed to have been erased.

But how was it possible? It was just sports highlights and a boring sideline interview—something TV viewers across the nation watched on a daily basis. *Oh my God.* That had to be it.

My head felt dizzy, as if I were suffering from sunstroke, but it was the sudden onslaught of questions spinning through my brain. Was Elven glamour somehow enhanced by electronic signals? Satellites? The video on Emmy's computer seemed to have had the same effect, so maybe the glamour was strengthened by the internet as well.

And of course radio signals carried songs like Nox's to the world—perhaps they had a similar effect on music listeners. If it was true, that would explain how celebrity obsession and interest in fan pods were spreading like wildfire.

I had to tell Nox about this—get his take on it. Without any further thought for my attire, or lack thereof, I reached for the nearby deck ladder and climbed out of the water, turning my head in a scan of the area. Hopefully, he was still here.

When I found Nox's eyes, they were already on me. As he had before, he ran his gaze up and down my body, like he couldn't drag his eyes away. Maybe he was in disbelief that I was actually wearing such an embarrassing getup. *You and me both, buddy.*

I strode across the hot tile, intending to head for the bathroom in the pool house and send him a message to meet me there so we could talk in a secluded spot. But before I could get close, he'd already crossed the deck to meet me.

"*What* are you *wearing?*" he hissed. "Do you have *any* idea what kind of reaction you're causing over there?"

"It wasn't my choice. The house manager ordered me to wear this. But it doesn't even matter. We have more important things to talk about."

"Talk? How am I supposed to concentrate on conversation when you're parading around practically naked?"

"Well, stop looking. What are you even doing here anyway?"

"I had to make sure you were okay. Good thing I *am* here, too, because—"

Before he could finish, Reggie ran toward me and lowered his shoulder as if going in for a tackle. Instead, he scooped me off my feet and held me against his bare chest with one arm around my back and the other under my knees.

"Here's my new prize." He laughed out loud and started carrying me toward the bar like a doe he'd hunted and felled. "You looking for a drink, Southern Belle? Let me get you something—whatever you want, sweet thing. Hey Nils," he shouted to the bartender. "Get this lovely lady something blue to drink—with an umbrella."

He lowered my feet to the pavement but did not release me entirely. Instead, he kept his arm around my waist, his large hand covering my hip as he continued to steer me toward the tiki bar.

I had no choice but to go along. I couldn't see Nox anymore, but the other guys were clustered around the bar area. Their eyes dropped to my cleavage as we approached.

Even when I looked away, I still felt their lusty gazes on my body.

"Oh, here we go," said a blond surfer-dude looking guy. He *had* to be a male model. "Reggie's in rare form today. Look while you can boys—this one may not survive the night."

"She may not survive the next hour," said an actor I recognized, his English accent more pronounced than it was on screen. The other guys laughed and nodded.

"I call next if she does," one of them shouted.

Another one added with a note of sympathy, "She looks like a newbie. Look at those big eyes. Maybe you should lay off the kinky stuff this time—show her some mercy, eh Reg?"

The other men snickered as if the idea of Reggie showing mercy was somehow a joke.

"I'll show her the inside of my bedroom," he said with a swaggering grin. "And *then* I'll show her my—"

Nox stepped into our path, his posture tense, his face severe. His shoulders were back, fists clenched at his sides. He was blocking our way to the bar, and Reggie was not amused.

He straightened his back, emphasizing the height difference between him and Nox. "Hey man, what's the problem? You not having a good time at my pool party?"

"It's great," Nox ground out, never taking his eyes from me.

"Well, what then? You got a thing for this girl? 'Cause that's a mistake, man. That's not how things work. They're not like us, you know."

Nox froze a second, then his face relaxed and he took a half-step back, releasing a long breath. "No. I know. There's no problem."

"Good," Reggie said, a new challenge entering his voice. "Because I don't *like* problems. I *do* like my new toy, though." He pulled me in tightly to his side and nuzzled my neck. Then he slowly and deliberately licked my earlobe.

And Nox exploded into action.

He lunged at Reggie, catching him off-guard and knocking the larger, thicker man to the pool deck with a blow to the jaw.

I stumbled to the side as the other guys swarmed toward the fight, a couple of them reaching to pull Reggie back onto his feet and two others grabbing Nox's arms to restrain him and prevent him from attacking our party host a second time.

Reggie slowly got to his feet and then his huge arm was swinging through the air so quickly it was almost a blur. There was a loud crack as his fist connected with Nox's cheek. If not for the men holding his arms, I'm sure Nox would've dropped instantly.

There were delayed screams and flying questions as the girls caught wind of what was happening and began rushing in our direction. Within minutes, Nox, Reggie, and I were encircled by the alarmed faces of his fan pod members and the hardened expressions of all the Elven men.

What were you thinking? I asked Nox silently, blinking back tears at his swelling cheekbone and wondering if my desperation came through in the mind-to-mind communication. He was hurt. And his impulsive reaction had probably blown our cover. It might even prevent me from getting Emmy out of here tonight.

I couldn't just stand there and let him treat you like that. His eyes blazed as they roamed my face and body, looking for damage.

You should have—I could've handled it. And stop looking at me like that, I warned him. *We're already in enough trouble.*

"What the hell is wrong with you, man?" Reggie asked, rubbing one hand across his jaw. "You're lucky I don't beat your ass into tomorrow."

Nox stared him down, refusing to answer.

"I give you credit for having a pair—and a mean right hook—but you're gonna have some explaining to do when the Council hears about this."

Nox's eyes went wide with alarm and the sudden realization of how much he'd screwed up. "The Council?"

"Yeah. And Davis is in town tonight, so you get to face the council *and* the main man."

Davis was here? In L.A.? *Oh no.* On one hand I was glad he wasn't with Mom back home in Mississippi. On the other, this was very, very bad. Davis knew who I was—Mom had no doubt shown him pictures. He'd recently spent time in Altum, so he might recognize Nox, too.

The fact he was Vancia's adoptive father made me suspect he might already know what I was doing out here—not checking out a college as I'd told Mom, but masquerading as one of Nox's fan girls. If Vancia was on his side, she'd undoubtedly told him she saw me. Maybe that's why he'd come to California.

What would he do when he learned his own biological daughter was working *against* his fan pod system? What would he do when he found out Nox was trying to help me? I had to do something to stop this. Nox and I were not ready to face the leader of the Dark Elves.

"What should we do with him?"

"Take him in the house—put him in a guest room and put a guard at the door," Reggie ordered. "I'll let Davis know what's going on."

Nox's jaw clenched and he yanked his tightly-held arms, but he was outsized and outnumbered. He had no choice but to go along with the linebacker-types as they led him into Reggie's mansion.

Our host looked around at the audience of bewildered girls and frowned. "What's the matter with you all? This is a party. Get back in the water. Let's have some drinks, Nils. And turn the volume back up on the TV."

Ah—so Reggie knew how it worked. He was clearly in the inner circle of Dark Elven society in a way Nox wasn't. He probably knew all kinds of things that could help us. One thing he didn't know about—at least not until he

247

talked to Davis—was my Elven heritage. I had to act now, before it was too late and I lost the element of surprise.

I stepped close to him again and placed a hand on one of his bulging biceps. The other I let rest on his abdomen as I turned my chin up and gazed into his face. "Didn't you promise to show me your room?" I asked in the most seductive voice I could muster.

I sounded ridiculous to myself, but it seemed to work for Reggie. He looked down at me with fiery eyes and a lewd grin. "Oh yeah—I believe I did." He slid a hand into his pocket and pulled out his cell phone. "I need to make one call first."

Dang it. I knew who he was planning to call—Davis. I couldn't let that happen.

I grabbed the phone from his hand and dropped it into the front of my suit. "No. I want all your attention."

His eyes flared in appreciation, either for my spunk or the new location of his phone. "Well, well. You *are* a surprise. Come on then, baby."

Letting his hand drop to one of my butt cheeks, he steered me toward the back door of his house.

I sure hope I know what I'm doing here. My stomach trembled as we entered the house and walked through the hallways toward Reggie's quarters. This was a risky move. I wasn't all that confident in my glamour skills, and my seductress act had clearly gotten Reggie fired up. I had to be careful. *This* Dark Elf was definitely not Nox, someone who cared about me and my feelings and what was best for me.

This guy was accustomed to using girls, taking whatever he wanted and then throwing them away. I might be very sorry I'd invited myself into his suite instead of using the fight as an opportunity to escape.

But what choice did I have? Not only was Emmy Reggie's captive here, now Nox was his prisoner as well.

CHAPTER TWENTY-FOUR
CELLS

The suite doors closed behind us, the guards banished to the outside. Reggie turned and gave me a hungry look. "Why don't we start with a game of find-the-phone?" he suggested.

I reached into the front of my suit bottom and plucked it out, depriving him of the chance. Grinning, I tossed the phone onto an overstuffed chair. "Why don't we talk first?" I was about to find out whether I actually had the Sway or not. If the answer was no, this would be a very *short* conversation.

"Talk?" Reggie said, blinking several times in succession.

"Yes, I'm feeling a little shy, and I'd like to get to know you a bit before we do anything else."

He laughed out loud. "You are an odd one, aren't you? Hot—but odd. Reggie's not interested in talking. I can talk to my teammates. I can talk to my fans. Now get over here and let me take you out of that rubber band you're wearing."

Oh no. It's not working. I needed to try harder. I needed to focus and fully embrace my Elven side, to let the Sway come forth—now or never.

I walked right up to Reggie and stood in front of him, looking him in the eye. "We *are* going to talk. In fact, you're feeling pretty tired from today's practice, and you'd like to sit down in that chair right now. You couldn't stand any more even if you wanted to, and you certainly don't have the energy to fool around."

Reggie stared back for a few seconds then he shook his head and his eyelids began to droop. "Whew, baby. Tell you what—I am beat from training camp today. Mind if I sit down a few minutes?"

I smiled at him sweetly. "No. Go ahead. Get comfortable."

He walked over to the chair and collapsed into it, leaning back and stretching. He gave me a rueful grin. "Hard workout today. I don't think I even have the energy to fool around. Want to just talk?"

Energized by my apparent success, I dove into the interrogation. "I'd love to. Why don't you tell me about The High Council?" At this, he flinched. Maybe I'd pushed for too much too soon. "Or about Davis? He sounds like a scary guy."

"You have no idea. You do not mess with that dude. The Council's no picnic either, but I'd much rather deal with them."

"So you're not on the Council then."

"No."

"Do you know what they want?"

"What they want? What do you mean?"

Re-focusing my concentration, I leaned into the Sway, urging Reggie to tell me everything. "I mean the fan pods. What do they want with them? What are they for?"

"Oh—well, they're for us to enjoy. And they make us look good to the other humans. They help us get our message out."

"And what's the message?"

"That we're good. That we're superior and deserve to be served, to be worshipped, as it should be, as it was." He sounded like he was reciting some mantra he'd been forced to memorize in elementary school.

"They don't even know you're not human."

"They will. Soon they will."

"Do you remember when things were like that?"

"Me? No. I'm not that old. I've only lived one hundred fifteen years. But I have many friends who do remember. Alfred is one of them."

"Alfred Frey? Your agent?"

"Yeah. Alfred knows how it was. He says it'll be that way again, and Davis will make sure it happens."

"Why do you have the fan pods watch TV all the time? Watch your videos online? What does it do?"

"It helps, you know, with the glamour. Alfred says the signals magnify the glamour—he discovered it in the fifties, when TV was invented. Not that many people had TV's then. But now... now people basically carry them around with them. We can glamour them almost twenty-four-seven now that so many humans carry smart phones and use them all day and night. It's getting flat-out easy. He says the plan may be accomplished even sooner than expected."

"The plan?"

Reggie opened his mouth to answer me, but then the doors to his suite flew open and Ingrid walked in.

"Excuse me, but we have a situation."

Reggie stood, his face looking groggy, perhaps from the leftover Sway I'd laid on him. "What is it?"

"Your *guest*—Nox—is uncontrollable. He's tearing up the room we're holding him in. He broke a window and nearly jumped from the second floor trying to escape. He's insisting on seeing this girl."

"Her?"

"Yes. He was particularly adamant that she not visit your suite."

"I don't give a crap what he says. She's mine—he traded her. He's a punk anyway."

Her face turned apprehensive. "He may be more than that."

"What do you mean?"

"He says when we learn his real identity, we're going to be sorry. He suggested he somehow outranks you."

"What the hell does that mean? He can't be more than twenty years old."

"I'm not sure, but he told me in the—" Here she glanced at me and stopped herself. "He communicated it in a way that I'm certain he's telling the truth. You know what I'm talking about."

"Oh. Well, go back and find out what he's talking about."

"I'd love to, but he's refusing to explain until he sees this one." She pointed at me.

Reggie glanced at me, back to Ingrid, and then back at me again. Shrugging, he said, "All right then. I'll talk to him. Come on, girl. Let's go see your boyfriend."

I followed Reggie and Ingrid as they moved swiftly through the halls to an elevator that carried us two stories beneath the mansion's first floor. They led me down an unadorned hallway lined with doors. Storage rooms, maybe? At the end of the hall, Ingrid pushed a key into the lock of one door. Looking back over her shoulder, she explained, "We moved him down here to keep him from escaping—or breaking his legs trying to."

When she opened the door, I saw Nox, sitting on the floor, his hands behind his back, head hanging between his knees. He lifted his head as we entered. His eyes went immediately to me.

"Ryann," he cried, his voice hoarse.

"Nox, are you okay?" I tried to go to him, but Reggie grabbed my shoulders and held me.

"You get your hands off her you son of a—if I find out you've touched her, harmed her in any way—"

"Okay, okay, sparky. Your girlie's fine. Man, what happened to that pretty voice of yours? You sound rough."

Ingrid turned to Reggie and rolled her eyes. "He's been singing at the top of his lungs, trying to glamour the guards. It almost worked, too. One of them unlocked the door and he was halfway down the hallway when I came up to investigate with Olar—who's completely tone-deaf." She grinned an evil grin. "Another reason we put him here below ground. The sound waves don't carry."

Now that she mentioned it, I looked around the room. It contained a low cot, a wall sink and a toilet. Nothing else. I'd never been in a prison, but the room looked like the cells I'd seen in movies and on TV. Why on earth would Reggie need a room like this in his mansion? And those other doors I'd seen in the hallway, assuming they were storage rooms—were they all cells, too? *Soundproof* rooms?

"So—here's your girl. Now what's this about you being somebody special? You're a noob. You just got to town, and you ain't even had your twentieth birthday yet."

"I'm new to town because I've been living with the Light Elves for the past five years—in Altum."

Reggie and Ingrid blinked in obvious shock and shared a worried glance.

"Don't you get it?" He laughed, though the subject matter wasn't the least bit funny. "I *work* for the Dark

Council. I've been a sleeper agent for the past five years, waiting to fulfill my mission."

"And what was your mission?"

"Killing King Ivar, of course. I killed him. And now I've come home to receive my reward."

CHAPTER TWENTY-FIVE
A RIDE YOU CAN'T REFUSE

The air left my lungs so fast I felt dizzy. Nox was confessing to Ivar's murder? Was he bluffing in order to get them to let him go? Or could it be true?

I tried extending my emotional E.Q. toward him, but all I got was a blend of adrenaline and hope—and what was it—victory? His face certainly wasn't giving anything away. If I were going on body language alone, I'd say he was telling the truth.

Nox struggled to get to his feet, gave Ingrid and Reggie a confident smile, then turned his back to us so we could see his cuffed hands. "Now, if you don't mind releasing me, *I* need to call Davis."

Reggie and Ingrid turned to each other, clearly confused. I read fear as the dominant emotion. They were afraid of Davis, particularly of disappointing him. Nox had either come up with a brilliant ruse during his captivity in this small room, or he was finally copping to the truth to get himself out of an uncomfortable position.

"He *was* in Altum," Reggie said. "I saw him at the Assemblage. He was there on the day of the murder before we all high-tailed it out of there."

It was enough to convince Ingrid to step forward, pull a small key from her pocket, and unlock Nox's handcuffs. He spun around and grinned at us all, rubbing his wrists.

"That's better. I'll be sure to tell Davis how reasonable you both were. Now, if I may have my phone?" He extended a hand toward Ingrid.

She must have put his phone in her purse because she turned her head to glance at the bag she'd dropped right inside the doorway.

As soon as she looked away from him, Nox sprang into motion. In what seemed like one lightning-fast move, he grabbed the open handcuffs from Ingrid and slapped one onto Reggie's wrist. Then twisting Reggie's other hand behind him, he clamped on the other cuff. Before the larger, stronger man even realized what was happening, Nox had kicked his feet out from under him, knocking him down. Reggie's head hit the bare floor with a crack, and he was out cold.

Ingrid's eyes flew open wide. Not a small woman herself, she was still no physical match for Nox. She turned toward the door. *She's going to run away.* But she only crossed the room to her purse. Plunging her hand into it, she came out with a gun.

"There will be no more of that," she said, turning back around. Nox started toward her and she pulled the trigger, firing just to the side of him. The shot left my ears ringing and a hole in the wall behind Nox. He froze in place.

"That's right. It's loaded," she said with a triumphant grin.

"You won't shoot me—I work for the council," Nox warned, taking a cautious half-step toward her.

She hesitated for a second then turned the gun toward me. "You're right—I'm not going to shoot you—not before I find out the truth about you. But I will shoot your little human here. I have no problem with that. And she's rather important to you for some reason, isn't she?"

Nox stopped in place again. "This has nothing to do with her. Let's go upstairs, contact Davis, and leave her out of it."

Ingrid took a quick step toward me and grabbed my arm, pressing the gun against my back. "I don't think so. I think we'll take her with us." She nodded toward him then at the door. "You first, big guy."

Nox glared at her. "I swear, if you hurt her..." But he obeyed her order, walking to the door and out into the hallway. He stopped in front of the elevator.

"No. Take the stairs," Ingrid said.

Nox opened the door to the stairwell and went inside.

Don't worry. I heard his voice inside my head. *I'll get us out of this.*

Be careful.

Once he glanced back over his shoulder and I thought he might try to fight Ingrid off, but I guessed the sight of the pistol barrel to my side changed his mind. As we climbed I gave the Sway a try. It had worked on Reggie. Maybe it would work on her.

She was behind me, but I pictured Ingrid's face. Concentrating as hard as I could, I willed her to drop the gun and let us go. No luck. The nose of the pistol pressed every bit as firmly against my back. Maybe fear was messing with my ability. Maybe Ingrid wasn't as susceptible to the Sway. We came out of the stairwell in the hall between the kitchen and butler's pantry.

"Keep walking," she instructed. "We're going outside now—through the front. Then we'll be driving to the Capitol Records tower. You want to go before the Dark Council so badly—you'll get your wish."

I started to become hopeful. If it was just the three of us with Nox driving, I might be able to overcome Ingrid at some point or surprise her and get the gun away from her. She wouldn't be able to keep it on us both so easily in the vehicle. I liked our odds once we were away from this house and the Elven bodyguards.

My hopes sank as two large men met us at the front door. Ingrid must have called them.

"Put this on," she ordered, tossing me a cover-up—whose, I wasn't sure.

I didn't complain. I had no desire to face the Council—or anyone—in that outrageous swimsuit. I slipped the garment over my head just before Ingrid shoved me toward one of the guards.

"Put them in the trunk."

The man nodded and gripped my shoulder. The other guy grabbed Nox's arms and pinned them behind him, forcing him out the front door.

We've got to do something here, Ry. Though he communicated silently mind-to-mind, Nox sounded worried. *We can't let them take us to the tower.*

Because you lied about killing Ivar?

He didn't answer my question directly. *Because I've been lying about my name. And once your father learns who I really am, I'm pretty sure he's going to kill me.*

My heart seized. He was right. Vancia's real father had been the leader of the Dark Elves. Nox's father was second-in line to the throne. Davis ascended to leadership when they both died in the plane crash. And apparently he'd told everyone Nox and his mother had died in the crash as well.

But now Nox was no longer a boy—he was eighteen—a man in the Elven world. And that made him a threat. Perhaps Davis had hoped the Dark heir would never re-surface. Perhaps Nox's mother had convinced him—insisting even under duress or torture—her son was dead and not a threat to his royal aspirations.

But if we walked into that iconic Hollywood building and Nox confronted him, Davis would know his time was up—and he'd likely be facing murder charges as well as losing his position as ruler. He'd already proved he was willing to kill to capture the throne. He'd certainly do it again to keep it.

It seemed impossible this guy was my natural father. What had Mom been thinking?

The guards marched us toward the waiting Bentley, the one escorting me reaching it first. As he pressed the key fob to pop the trunk open, I tried again to use my persuasion glamour. *You don't want to do this. Let go.*

His grip on me released, and his brow furrowed in confusion. I'm sure he wondered where the heck the voice had come from. He must have thought it was Ingrid because he looked back toward her, wearing a quizzical expression. I set to work on Nox's guard.

Release him immediately.

His grip also loosened, and Nox fought to break free.

"What are you doing, you idiots? Get them! Put them in." Ingrid rushed toward us, brandishing the gun again.

The Sway broken, the guards again grabbed me and Nox and followed her orders, shoving him roughly into the trunk and me in on top of him. Nox put a palm over my head and pulled it down toward his chest as the lid slammed closed.

"You're okay," he whispered, gripping me tightly and pressing a kiss into my hair. "You're okay."

"Not really," I said. "I'm *really* claustrophobic. We've got to figure out a way out of here"

"No kidding. This isn't on my top ten list of places to be. And neither is a coffin."

"What are we going to do?" My question was followed by an involuntary whimper.

He petted my head, speaking close to my ear. "I don't know. I don't know yet, baby. We're kind of on our own. We don't have any friends out here."

And then it hit me, a tiny spark of hope. "Yes we do."

"Do what?"

"Have friends. Lad and Vancia are still in town. Well, he *was* our friend—and she was your friend a long time ago. They aren't scheduled to fly out until tonight."

"But even if they could help us, how are we supposed to contact them? Ingrid took my phone. Even if I had one, I don't have a number for Vancia—I'm sure Lad has no phone."

"Can't you call him—the Elven way?" I asked.

"No. I told you—you're the only one I've ever heard from a distance. Lad and I don't have that kind of connection."

"Maybe... maybe I can try calling him."

Nox stiffened under me. "It's not going to work. You're not together anymore. You said he didn't want you anymore." His tone was bruised and adamant.

But hurt feelings didn't matter right now. This was a matter of life and death. And he was probably right. Lad and I had only begun to work on our mind-to-mind communication, and we'd never even tried it long distance. Now that our attachment had been severed, it probably wouldn't work, but what else could we do?

"It's worth a try, right? It's the only chance we've got."

"I guess so," he grumbled.

"All right then. Be quiet and let me concentrate."

And I did. I concentrated like I never had before in my life, taxing every brain cell I had to remember the details of Nox's lessons in mental communication. I opened my mind and allowed myself to relive those uncomfortable, exciting moments when we'd made a real breakthrough, and the sense of desperation I'd felt on the bus when I'd cried out for him and he'd heard me.

Then I opened my heart. And I drew on the deep connection I'd had with Lad. Taking off the emotional clamps, I finally allowed my feelings to flow free, allowed myself to feel all the love I'd ever had for him, before he rejected me, before he'd pushed me into Nox's arms and then showed up with his fiancée.

I gave free reign to the painful sweet feelings I'd suppressed and let them envelope me once again with no concern for the future consequences. My heart felt nearly crushed from the fierce weight of my love for him, but I pressed on, drawing on the pain to empower me as I called to him.

Lad, I need you. I'm in trouble. Nox and I are in great danger. Please help if you can. We're being taken to the Capitol Records Tower. We don't have much time.

I had no idea if he could hear me, whether he'd even respond if he did. Even if he got the message and wanted to respond, would Vancia allow him to come to our aid— or would she try to stop him? She was Davis's adopted daughter. She might be a sleeper agent like Nox had claimed to be. Or perhaps she was just another innocent victim of Davis's schemes. Perhaps she truly cared for her fiancé and would do anything he asked. For now all we could do was hope and pray and wait.

"What did you say to him?" Nox's voice was guarded and filled with hurt. Hope and pray and wait—and apparently pout.

"I called for help. I told him where we were going. Why? Don't tell me you're jealous."

"You bet I am."

I let out a weary sigh. "Don't you want them to come help us?"

"I do, and I don't. If they don't show up, we're screwed. If they do—if they do, that means he heard you, and the emotional connection between the two of you is still there."

"It doesn't matter, Nox. He doesn't want me anymore. If he comes, it's only because he doesn't want us falling into the hands of Davis and the Dark Council."

"Well, we don't have a chance anyway. These guys guarding us are effing strong. And I'm willing to bet the Capitol Records building is one of the most closely guarded places on the planet. Once we're inside those doors, it would be easier to extract us from the White House."

"Well, we'd better hope they show up before we get inside then. Let's not talk. We're using up all our oxygen, and my claustrophobia's getting worse."

"Fine." His hands clamped around my face, pulling it to his. His lips covered mine and moved in a frenzy of desperation and passion. Like he couldn't wait another second to taste my mouth. Like it might be his last chance to do so.

CHAPTER TWENTY-SIX
THE DARK KING

The car stopped after what seemed like an eternity. We could hear muffled voices and then the thump of doors as Ingrid and the guards got out of the car.

And then there was blinding daylight and fresh air as the restrictive sheet of metal above us lifted. Glorious, because we were no longer trapped in the cramped trunk. Terrible, because there, looming above us, was the iconic circular Capitol Records Building, shaped like an old-fashioned record player with stacked disks and a needle sticking out of the top. I'd read the light atop the needle flashed Morse code for Hollywood twenty-four hours a day.

I blinked and looked around the parking lot as I was pulled from the trunk by one of the Elven guards. The action movie rescue scene I'd been hoping for was apparently not going to happen. The lot was full of high-end cars, but not a single person was in sight who might call 9-1-1 on our behalf or intervene in any way.

Holding us securely, the guards followed Ingrid, marching us toward the building and the doom awaiting us inside.

And that's when a shiny black limo sped into the parking lot and skidded to a stop near us. The back door sprang open, and Lad came out at full speed, crashing into the guard who held me and knocking him on his backside.

The front passenger door opened and the driver leaned over the seat toward me, motioning for me to get in. I ran to him and slid inside. Looking back over my shoulder, I saw Vancia seated in the back.

"Thank you for coming," I said to her.

She gave me a withering look before turning her attention back to the scene outside her window. "I didn't come for *you*."

Now Lad was grappling with the second guard, the one who was restraining Nox. The guard he'd attacked first was getting to his feet behind Lad, and Ingrid was fishing in her purse, no doubt for the gun.

I jiggled the door handle furiously but it refused to open. The driver must have locked it. He gripped the steering wheel, staring straight ahead—glamoured, no doubt. He must have been told not to leave the car—his primary job to provide us all a means of escape.

"Let me out," I screamed at him. Then I turned back to Vancia. "Do something. They're going to hurt him."

She let out a bitter laugh as she opened her door. "Which boyfriend are you concerned about most, I wonder?" Then she got out.

I beat on the window of the passenger side, desperate to help. "Lad—watch out—she has a gun," I cried as Ingrid drew the weapon from her purse and aimed it at him.

Nox broke free from his distracted captor and leapt toward her, coming between her and Lad as she squeezed the trigger.

"No!" My scream filled the car.

Nox's body jerked back as the bullet made contact. He hit the pavement in front of Lad, going to his knees and then one hip, clutching his left shoulder. Ingrid grinned and aimed the gun again, this time at Lad.

Vancia's command was loud and authoritative as she strode toward the group. "Stop. Don't shoot either one of them."

I could tell Ingrid and her guards recognized Vancia on site because their eyes went wide and they all fell back a few steps.

"Let me out, let me out, let me out!" I demanded, directing my own glamour at the stoic driver.

Finally, he hit the unlock button, allowing me to exit the car and run over to where Nox now lay on the ground.

"Oh my God. You're shot," I said through tears. "Where were you hit? Does it hurt?"

What a dumb question. His face was white with pain, and tiny beads of sweat covered his skin. "He heard you," he said weakly. "He heard you."

Nox's eyes closed, though he was still breathing. Maybe he'd passed out from the pain. I looked up at the Elves surrounding me. "He needs an ambulance. Someone call 9-1-1," I demanded.

Ingrid snarled at me. "Shut up, *human*. He'll be *taken care* of soon enough."

Now Vancia spoke, and her tone was imperious. "You'd better hope so, *house manager*. You've just shot the heir to the Dark Throne."

Ingrid's face lost all color, contorting with alarm. "What do you mean? Your father—"

"My *father* was merely holding the position while the search continued for the missing heir. And he is found."

Ingrid and the two guards dropped to their knees and bowed as Vancia continued. Gesturing toward Nox, who lay bleeding in a Los Angeles parking lot at the corner of Hollywood and Vine, she said, "This is Nox Jerrik, son of Gavin Jerrik—and he is our *true* leader. He *is* the Dark King."

Epilogue

Lad and I crossed the tarmac at LAX toward a private jet belonging to Davis Hart. After instructing Ingrid and her henchmen to let us go, Vancia had called the pilot and told him to fly us non-stop to the Oxford airport near Deep River tonight. She wouldn't be joining us. Neither would Nox.

I didn't know where Davis was or what Vancia had told her *Pappa*. I wasn't even sure he knew I was in L.A. for anything other than a summer vacation and some college visits, the cover story I'd given Mom.

What he *would* know soon enough, if he didn't already, was that Nox was alive and well—and a deadly threat to his rule. And he'd know his adoptive daughter Vancia had betrayed him by choosing her childhood friend over the man who'd raised her.

All *I* knew was I'd failed. I'd come out to L.A. to save Emmy from enslavement in a fan pod, and now I was

271

leaving without her. And without Nox, who'd risked everything to help me.

"What do you think will happen to him?" I asked Lad as we watched our bags being loaded onto the Lear jet.

"He'll be all right," he reassured me. "He's smart. And now he's got Vancia on his side. She's smart, too, and she's furious at Davis for pretending to care for her when all he really cared about was protecting his own interests. She'll make sure the Dark Council sees Nox and hears his story. I'm sure it's already happened. By now they know the validity of his claim to the Dark Throne. There's nothing Davis can do to him."

"Maybe not." I sniffed. "But what will the *Dark Throne* do to him?"

"Try not to worry about it. It's out of your control. For now, concentrate on your mom and your grandma and father, on going home."

I nodded. He was right. My mom might be the only person I *could* help. I couldn't help Nox. I couldn't help all those poor girls stuck in fan pods around the world, being used, sometimes tortured by Dark Elves who saw their lives as less valuable than Elven lives, as toys, as disposable. Lad didn't want or need my help—he was going home to his people, and he had an eternal future to look forward to with his perfect Elven bride.

The roar of an engine caught my ear. A car was speeding toward us across the tarmac. I darted a glance at Lad, but he didn't seem alarmed. In fact, he smiled widely.

The car stopped. An obviously Elven driver got out and opened the back door. And Emmy emerged.

I looked back at Lad, who was beaming at me expectantly. "You knew? How did you…"

"Go on," he said, nudging me toward my long lost friend.

I ran to Emmy, reaching her and locking her in a death squeeze.

"Ryann? What are you doing here?"

I didn't bother to answer her question. She obviously didn't remember seeing me at Reggie's house. I'd have plenty of time on the airplane to explain. "I'm so happy to see you," I told her. "I missed you so much."

"I missed you, too," she said, still looking bewildered. "But I'm kinda bummed out."

"Why?"

"I got kicked out of the fan pod. Ingrid came into my room a little while ago with this bitchy blonde girl, and they told me to pack." Her face crumpled into teary disappointment. "My dream is over, Ryann."

I hugged her again, filled with a mixture of sympathy and sweet relief. "Yeah, but Emmy—your life—" I got choked up and had to start again. "Your life is just beginning."

Unconvinced, she trudged tiredly up the boarding stairs into the plane. I followed her, but stopped midway, turning back to Lad. His extraordinary green eyes were now level with mine.

"I get why Vancia saved Nox—and you, of course. But why did she help Emmy? Why help me?"

Those eyes were soft and glistening now, staring back at me. "Ryann, there's so much you don't know. So much I couldn't tell you, things I had to keep hidden in my heart."

My own heart trembled at the look on his face, the tender sound of his voice. "What things?" I whispered.

Lad lifted a finger and stroked my cheek softly. "Let's go home, and I'll tell you."

THE END

AFTERWORD

Thank you for reading HIDDEN HEART, Book Two of the Hidden Trilogy. If you enjoyed it, please consider leaving a review on Goodreads and wherever you purchased your copy. Reviews help other readers find great books!

The Hidden Trilogy continues with Book 3, HIDDEN HOPE, available now. To learn about upcoming releases from Amy Patrick, sign up for her newsletter. You will only receive notifications when new titles are available and about special price promotions. You may also occasionally receive teasers, excerpts, and extras from upcoming books. Amy will never share your contact information with others.

And check out http://www.hiddentrilogy.com/ for more information on the Hidden series.

You're invited to follow Amy on Twitter at @amypatrickbooks https://twitter.com/AmyPatrickBooks, and visit her website at www.amypatrickbooks.com. You can also connect with her on Facebook https://www.facebook.com/AmyPatrickAuthor

ACKNOWLEDGMENTS

This is an important part of the book for me because without the people named here, HIDDEN HEART wouldn't exist.

First to you, my reader… thank you for giving my books a chance to entertain you and touch your heart.

Huge thanks go to my lovely editor Judy Roth for her wonderful work and to Cover Your Dreams for another beautiful cover.

I am forever grateful for my amazing critique partner, McCall, for her words of wisdom and huge heart. I'd be nowhere without my brilliant and hilarious Savvy Seven sisters and the Dauntless girls. Love and thanks to the rest of the fabulous Dreamweavers and my Lucky 13 sisters for their support, good advice, virtual Prosecco, cupcakes, and cabana boys. #teamworddomination.

I'm blessed to be "doing life" with some amazing friends. Love to Bethany, Chelle, Margie, and the real housewives of Westmoreland Farm. Special thanks to Mary and CM and Bria for all the great book (and life) talks.

To my first family for your unconditional love and the gift of roots and wings. And finally to the guys who make it all worthwhile—my husband and sons. And thank you to the rest of my friends and family for your support and for just making life good.

ABOUT THE AUTHOR

Amy Patrick grew up in Mississippi (with a few years in Texas thrown in for spicy flavor) and has lived in six states, including Rhode Island, where she now lives with her husband and two sons.

Amy has been a professional singer, a DJ, a voiceover artist, and always a storyteller, whether it was directing her younger siblings during hours of "pretend" or inventing characters and dialogue while hot-rollering her hair before middle school every day. For many years she was a writer of true crime, medical anomalies, and mayhem, working as a news anchor and health reporter for six different television stations. Then she retired to make up her own stories. Hers have a lot more kissing.

I love to hear from my readers. Feel free to contact me on Twitter and my Facebook page.

https://twitter.com/AmyPatrickBooks
https://www.facebook.com/AmyPatrickAuthor

And be sure to sign up for my newsletter and be the first to hear the latest news on Ryann, Lad, Nox, and the Hidden Trilogy.

The Hidden Trilogy

Hidden Deep

Hidden Heart

Hidden Hope

The Sway- A Hidden Novella

Other Books by Amy Patrick

Channel 20 Something

Still Yours (20 Something, Book 2)

Still Me (20 Something, Book 3)

Still Beautiful (20 Something, Book 4)

Still Waiting- coming soon

51277498R00170

Made in the USA
Middletown, DE
01 July 2019